SPECIAL MESSAGE TO READERS

This book is published under the auspices of

THE ULVERSCROFT FOUNDATION

(registered charity No. 264873 UK)

Established in 1972 to provide funds for research, diagnosis and treatment of eye diseases. Examples of contributions made are: —

A new Children's Assessment Unit at Moorfield's Hospital, London.

•

Twin operating theatres at the Western Ophthalmic Hospital, London.

•

A Chair of Ophthalmology at the University of Leicester.

•

The establishment of a Royal Australian College of Ophthalmologists "Fellowship".

You can help further the work of the Foundation by making a donation or leaving a legacy. Every contribution, no matter how small, is received with gratitude. Please write for details to:

**THE ULVERSCROFT FOUNDATION,
The Green, Bradgate Road, Anstey,
Leicester LE7 7FU, England.
Telephone: (0116) 236 4325**

**In Australia write to:
THE ULVERSCROFT FOUNDATION,
c/o The Royal Australian College of
Ophthalmologists,
27, Commonwealth Street, Sydney,
N.S.W. 2010.**

I've travelled the world twice over,
Met the famous: saints and sinners,
Poets and artists, kings and queens,
Old stars and hopeful beginners,
I've been where no-one's been before,
Learned secrets from writers and cooks
All with one library ticket
To the wonderful world of books.

© JANICE JAMES.

KEEPING IT DARK

Two women, born in the 1920s, related, but of totally different backgrounds, start out in life knowing nothing about the existence of the other. Gradually, the elder of the two — jealous, bold and disastrously attractive to the opposite sex — makes some surprising discoveries, which awaken in her an obsessive desire to destroy the unenlightened younger one. Set in the West Country at the end of the First World War, the story probes the eternal question: how much is an individual's make-up due to nature or to nurture?

Books by Pamela Street
in the Ulverscroft Large Print Series:

PAMELA STREET

◆

KEEPING IT DARK

Complete and Unabridged

ULVERSCROFT
Leicester

First published in Great Britain in 1994 by
Robert Hale Limited
London

First Large Print Edition
published 1996
by arrangement with
Robert Hale Limited
London

British Library CIP Data

Street, Pamela, *1921* -
Keeping it dark.—Large print ed.—
Ulverscroft large print series: general fiction
1.English fiction—20th century
I. Title
823.9'14 [F]

ISBN 0–7089–3511–7

Published by
F. A. Thorpe (Publishing) Ltd.
Anstey, Leicestershire
Set by Words & Graphics Ltd.
Anstey, Leicestershire
Printed and bound in Great Britain by
T. J. Press (Padstow) Ltd., Padstow, Cornwall

This book is printed on acid-free paper

Part One

Part One

1

"WHAT will you write for the notice on the gate, Doctor?"

Sidney Forman looked at the woman opposite him. Her expression gave nothing away. She was, as always, completely composed, no flicker of anxiety in the dark, slightly hooded eyes, no sign of fatigue, as she sat, still and upright, her black hair swept back into a severe bun, seemingly only concerned with the requirements of the moment.

"Your father is weaker, Miss Gertrude. I fear that . . . " he hesitated.

"He is failing." She finished the statement for him, in that quick terse manner he knew so well.

"Yes. I shall have to tell the truth. The village will expect no less."

"Of course."

"Your brother . . . ?" Dr Forman continued.

For the first time, the rector's daughter

3

appeared slightly disconcerted. "Claud is very busy, Doctor. As you know, he is working in the King's secretariat. He has never been too strong, especially since the wound to his leg. And besides, every effort is being made to reduce the risk of Spanish 'flu affecting the staff at the Palace."

"But he is your father's only son. The rector is past the infectious stage, but his heart has been affected by broncho-pneumonia as well as the toxin." Sidney Forman could feel his anger rising. "I think you should send for Claud," was all he now said, as he pulled out some writing-paper from his bag, preparatory to penning the notice about the condition of the rector of Netherford, which his daughter had requested. Then he stood up.

Gertrude rose also and took it from him with a curt nod of thanks. Gratitude had never been her strong point. As he left the rectory, well wrapped up against the chill winter wind, Sidney Forman had no means of knowing whether she would do as he suggested. Ever since Gertrude had been a child she had been an enigma to him. He was not surprised that, at the age of thirty-two, she was still unmarried. The only person for whom he had ever known her show affection was her brother, nine years her junior; and even that, Sidney felt, was unnatural, as if she had channelled whatever maternal instincts she might have had on to her dashing good-looking younger sibling. He supposed that he ought to make some allowance for the fact that, after the rector's wife had died of septicaemia in 1910, Gertrude had taken on the role of mistress of Netherford Rectory with extraordinary competence, if with no actual show of enthusiasm or warmth of feeling. But she had certainly mothered Claud and Sidney had never forgotten how, in an unguarded moment, she had almost broken down with relief when she had heard that he had been wounded, but not too seriously, in the second battle of Arras in March 1918 and had been sent home to be invalided out of the army altogether.

This had probably helped the young man to secure his present position, Sidney Forman reflected, as he climbed into his pony trap and his faithful groom/gardener and man of all works, Fred Penny, took up the reins. Claud had been able to get well ahead of his contemporaries who, after the armistice the following November, had found it hard to find suitable occupations; although the doctor could not also help feeling, a little cynically, that the boy's late mother's connections must have had more than a hand in Claud acquiring his present post at the Palace. The late Mrs Kimberley's father had been a baronet and her brother, Claud's uncle, had inherited the title.

There was no doubt in Sidney Forman's mind that the rector was the best of the bunch. The Reverend George Herbert Kimberley was a good man. He had always done his duty by his family and his flock. Now that he was dying it seemed incomprehensible to the doctor that his only daughter was procrastinating about sending for his only son.

As the trap turned into Pennyfarthing Lane, Sidney saw, out of the corner of his eye Gertrude, swathed in the black scarlet-lined cloak she had worn as a

VAD, stooping to insert his bulletin in the small photo frame which hung on the rectory gate. Many a local inhabitant would, he knew, read it before the day was out. And the ones who couldn't read would get others to do so for them and learn that: *The Reverend Mr Kimberley passed a restless night. It is feared that his condition has deteriorated. Signed Sidney James Forman, MB. January 6th, 1919.*

The doctor was not to know that Gertrude, on returning indoors, was hesitating a little in the hall, debating uneasily in her mind whether or not she should, after all, take his advice. If it had simply been her mother who was ill, she would have had no such compunction about putting off sending a telegram. The late Mrs Kimberley had never shown much outward affection towards her children and this state of affairs was reciprocated. But her father . . . Gertrude thought perhaps she should do as the doctor had advised. Deep down, she knew, as Sidney Forman knew only too well, that George Kimberley was a good man, one of the best. She wished she could have been more like him. But, in a curiously matter-of-fact way, she had accepted the fact she was not and that had seemed to be the end of the matter. She did not think she would ever marry, although she was aware that she was by no means averse to enjoying the obvious regard some men showed for her quick-wittedness and conversational skills. As for any maternal instinct, Claud more than fulfilled that, while other people — and things — fulfilled her less ordinary desires.

The thought came to her that if she simply wrote a letter to her brother, he would get it in London the following day. Then, if her father passed away before his son had time to reach Netherford, at least she would have done her duty, if not with quite the celerity for which Dr Forman might have hoped. She was about to go to her desk in the drawing-room, when the nurse who had been attending her father came swiftly down the stairs. One look at her face sent all thought of a letter out of Gertrude's mind.

She followed Nurse Everett upstairs and into her father's bedroom, pulling aside the sheet that had been doused in disinfectant at the start of the rector's illness, as a precaution against the risk of infection to the rest of the household and which still hung by the door. Gertrude had come to the conclusion that they were all, by now, probably immune. She herself had never been as frightened of catching Spanish 'flu as she was scared of having to perform any ministrations to her sick father. She might have been a part-time VAD in the war, but her duties had been confined to Netherford Manor, which had been turned into an officers' convalescent home. Here, she had carefully been able to avoid any of the undesirable tasks which she knew had befallen some young women of her acquaintance, such as emptying bedpans and dressing wounds in the emergency hospitals. Gertrude believed, without a shred of contrition or doubt, that her own special contribution to the war effort had lain in cheering up and conversing with men of her own class and intellectual level.

Now, as she looked down on her dying father, noted the blueness round the lips, heard the faint but laboured breathing, saw the thin white hand plucking at the bedspread which, had she had any natural spontaneous compassion, she would have taken in her own, she felt nothing other than a longing for his suffering to be over as soon as possible. Then, perhaps, her own life could begin.

Gertrude stayed but a few moments beside the bed. Then she went downstairs and into the drawing-room, where she pulled a cord which rang one of the numbered heavy bells in the kitchen quarters. Dora Penny, one of the two young house-parlourmaids and daughter of Dr Forman's general factotum, came quickly into the room, having already changed out of her blue morning uniform into a black serge afternoon dress, with white cap and apron.

Still busy at her desk, Gertrude scarcely looked up until she handed the girl an envelope addressed to the village postmistress. "I want you to take this down to Mrs Musselwhite at once, Dora," she said, her eyes noticing with satisfaction, despite the more important matters on her mind, her young employee's neat demeanour.

"Yes, ma'am."

"It's a telegram. It must go straight away." Gertrude unlocked a small tin cash box on her desk and withdrew a shilling. "This should more than cover the cost. Bring me the change as soon as you return."

"Yes, ma'am."

"And tell Cook I would like to see her."

"Yes, ma'am."

Dora Penny performed a quaint little bob and vanished.

A good girl, Gertrude thought. Well brought up. Personable. Getting very pretty. Coming along nicely under her and Cook's training. Must watch the child doesn't become too friendly with Dyer, the house boy. What a mercy it was that no one else in the household had gone down with 'flu. Perhaps there was something in Nurse Everett's idea of hanging up that sheet by the sick room door after all.

When Ethel Henstridge, the cook, came into the drawing-room, Gertrude was again busy writing, but this time the sheet of paper in front of her was

11

covered with notes: *Claud's bed to be aired. Shiner must be on standby to meet London train either at Castlebury or Netherford Halt. Steak and kidney. Apple tart. Ask farm for extra milk and cream* . . . Gertrude swivelled round in her chair and said, abruptly, "The rector is dying, Ethel. I have sent for Mr Claud."

Ethel Henstridge had already guessed the contents of the envelope which Dora had been told to take to the post office. She had been surprised that her mistress had not sent for the young master before but, of course, it was none of her business. She knew her place. She had also known, without having to be told by Nurse Everett, about the blue lips and the rector's inability to swallow the warm milk and brandy she had prepared earlier, that there was little hope. She had great affection for her employer and she was afraid she was now going to cry. Surreptitiously, she took out a handkerchief from the pocket of her voluminous white apron. She had been at the rectory since she was Dora's age, gradually working her way up to her present position. She had considered that the late Mrs Kimberley had been a good enough mistress, but it had always been the rector whom she and the whole of Netherford respected and, indeed, loved. As for Miss Gertrude, Ethel Henstridge could not feel any such sentiments, although as the years passed she had had to admit to a grudging admiration. The rector's daughter knew what she was about and the staff knew where they were with her. Even now, she seemed to have the whole situation completely under control although, after discussing the immediate needs, Ethel could not help feeling that it was acting with almost indecent haste when she started to talk about funeral arrangements.

"The Bishop," she heard Gertrude saying, "will be sure to conduct the service. We shall have to be prepared for many mourners returning to the rectory for tea." And even as her employer spoke, Ethel realised, guiltily, that she herself had begun to think about ham sandwiches and fairy cakes and how fortuitous it had been that she had bought a new black coat the last time she was in Castlebury.

13

2

CLAUD KIMBERLEY alighted at Netherford Halt and raised a hand in greeting to Shiner, the rector's trusted groom, who also performed many of the same tasks as the doctor's reliable jack-of-all-trades, Fred Penny.

Shiner, a rather less dour individual than Fred, quickly settled his passenger, together with his valise, into the pony trap, climbed into the driving seat, lightly flicked the whip at Bessie, who set off at a smart trot for Netherford Rectory. It wasn't, he felt, for him to say that the rector had passed away some hours ago. As long as Mr Claud didn't ask, then it was best left to Miss Gertrude to tell him. Of course, she should have sent for her brother earlier. They all knew that. As the short journey progressed, Shiner was relieved that his passenger seemed anxious to keep the conversation on a purely impersonal level.

It was getting on for midnight and bitterly cold. A white bright moon appeared fitfully now and then behind scudding clouds. Sparks from Bessie's hooves flew upwards as they struck the recently tar macadamised roadway. There were few lights in the windows as the trap rattled through the village but, once they turned into the drive of the rectory, there appeared to be several, both upstairs and down. As Shiner brought the trap to a halt by the front door, it opened at once and Gertrude stood there, silhouetted against the lamplit hall, her arms outstretched in a gesture of welcome which she was never known to use for anyone else.

Her brother clambered down from the trap and went towards her.

"Claud, my dear."

"Gertie."

He kissed her cheek. She wished he would not shorten her name, but she had long ago given up even tentatively trying to persuade him otherwise. After Shiner had placed his valise in the porch and brief goodnights were exchanged, the front door closed and brother and sister went into the drawing-room, where

Gertrude had sandwiches and a thermos of hot soup waiting by the well-stoked fire. As he watched her take out the cork top he asked the question which he had carefully refrained from asking Shiner.

"Is he dead?"

"Yes. Soon after Dr Forman's morning visit."

"Did he . . . suffer much?"

"Towards the end. But I hoped, even yesterday, that he was going to pull through."

"I'm sorry. You should have sent for me before."

She was silent. Then, after taking a sip or two of soup, he said, "Do you mind if I add a drop of brandy to this? It was a deuced cold journey."

"Of course." She left the room at once and returned with a decanter, noticing that more than a drop or two was then splashed into Ethel Henstridge's restorative broth.

"When will the funeral be?" he asked. "Or haven't you had time to think?"

"Oh, yes. On Friday. Bishop Robertson is officiating. Canon Armitage will assist him."

16

"What about notices?"

"I've already sent to *The Times* and the *Morning Post*, as well as all the locals. And, of course, I've sent wires to the relatives."

"My God, Gertie. You've thought of everything."

He was still standing, warming his tall backside at the fire. A live coal fell to the hearth. He turned quickly and kicked it into the ashes, ashes which it would be Dora Penny's job to remove in the morning, besides blacking the iron grate and shining the brass fire irons.

"Would you," Gertrude enquired, "like to see him? Nurse Everett has laid him out."

He gave a start. His pale handsome face took on an agonised look. "Not now, Gertie. I mean, well . . . tomorrow if you don't mind. It's been a hell of a day. Getting your telegram, asking for permission to leave, catching the first train I could. I'd just like to go to bed first."

"Of course. I quite understand." She picked up the thermos. "There's still some of this left."

17

"How about you?"

She shook her head. "I supped at the usual time."

He held out the giant-sized cup and saucer, then helped himself again to brandy, this time lavishly. He needs looking after, she thought, even more than I suspected. I shall have to put my plans into action as soon as possible.

The next morning they went together into the rector's bedroom. The Reverend George Kimberley's face was drawn back into an almost unrecognisable death mask. It was obvious to Gertrude that this was an ordeal for her brother and they stayed but a few moments. Then she excused herself on the grounds of having a lot to see to which was, indeed, true.

Claud, having been just too late to pay a final farewell to his father, now found himself somewhat at a loose end. There were three more days to fill in before the funeral. He wandered into the rector's book-lined study, noticed that it was, as always, tidy and uncluttered. The Reverend George Kimberley had been a methodical man. Claud supposed it was from him that his sister had inherited her astonishing organising capacity. He wondered what she would do now, where she would go. A lot depended on the will, but he felt sure it would be a fair one, both to himself and Gertie and his father's faithful retainers. Presumably, some minister from another parish would take on his duties, pending Gertrude's departure and the arrival of a new incumbent. It would seem strange no longer having Netherford Rectory as a family home. He had never thought before how much he might miss it. It had been a good background to his all but twenty years.

Yet he was aware that he liked being in London. He was finding it stimulating. There was so much going on. One could forget all the beastliness of the war. He was having a good time. There was no shortage of girls, nor nightclubs which were springing up all over the place. He had bought himself one of the new *His Master's Voice* gramophones and he could have listened to the latest jazz records forever. The trouble was that he was sharing a flat near Victoria with an old school friend, who was studying law. It was not an ideal arrangement. His friend was rather too earnest and, even if their surroundings had been a little more salubrious, he could not possibly entertain any lady friends there. But perhaps now he would be able to afford something better.

Claud shivered slightly. There was no fire in the study and he didn't like to go into the drawing-room, which Gertrude seemed to have commandeered like some general's headquarters. He decided the best thing to do would be to take himself off for a good long walk. He would head for Castlebury Rings where they had often gone as children, with their nursemaid. He believed the place still held a special attraction for Gertrude. He would work up an appetite for lunch which he knew, in spite of all the upheaval and comings and goings, would be a good one. Already the smell of Ethel Henstridge's steak and kidney pudding was permeating from the nether regions into the front of the house.

It was not until that evening, when Gertrude appeared to be less preoccupied and they were sitting quietly together by the drawing-room fire that she said, suddenly, "I've always understood from Mother's brother, Guy, that there are several grace and favour residences in Lower Grosvenor Place near the Royal Mews for those who work in an administrative capacity at the Palace."

"Why, yes," he replied, somewhat surprised, "for older members of the staff. Married ones, of long-standing."

"Not necessarily. Guy wasn't married when he first worked for the King. His mother ran Number 16 for him."

Claud frowned. He had always been aware that it was through his uncle, Sir Guy Hennessey, he had obtained his present position, one to be coveted. But he had ceased to feel guilty about his good fortune and had disregarded any allusions to nepotism. After all, had he not already served both King and Country, been wounded in so doing and received an honourable discharge from the army.

"Guy once told me," Gertrude went on, "that as long as a man had some suitable female relative to run his establishment, a wife was not a prerequisite."

Now, Claud simply stared at her. He realised what she was getting at. Several thoughts chased through his mind. A grace and favour home would be infinitely preferable to his present accommodation. Having Gertie to run it for him would absolve him from the slightest domestic problem. Moreover, he happened to know that old Sir Harry Wenham was due to retire and he and Lady Wenham would be moving shortly to another grace and favour home at Hampton Court. Of course, there would still be certain drawbacks living with Gertrude. Girls, for instance. It would be more than ever difficult to entertain any if heavily chaperoned by an older sister. Contrary to what might have been expected, he was still a virgin, longing for sexual experience. And what would happen when he did eventually marry? But he knew that there was a top flat in Sir Harry's house, because he had been to a dinner party there and was told it was occupied by an ancient nannie. He supposed that Gertrude could be shoved upstairs when a wife came on the scene.

Not for the first time did he wonder whether his sister was psychic when he heard her say, "I should be quite prepared to take a back seat, Claud, when you married. But I dare say that won't be for quite a few more years. Anyway, I thought, for what it is worth, I'd put this to you. You might like to think about it. Guy is, of course, coming to the funeral . . ."

23

3

GUY HENNESSEY did, indeed, come to the funeral, arriving the night before and occupying the best guest room at the rectory. He explained that, sadly, Lilly, his wife, was unable to accompany him because of increasing immobility due to arthritis.

On his cessation of duties at the Palace, thanks to his own substantial inheritance and his wife's dowry, he had left London altogether and retired to a large estate in the home counties. But, having no children, he had been only too pleased to help his late sister's son, by pulling whatever strings he could.

After his brother-in-law's funeral, he stood beside the grave in the churchyard, a large, florid, majestic figure, listening to the Bishop of Castlebury intoning *Earth to earth, ashes to ashes, in the sure and certain hope of the Resurrection to eternal life*, while at the same time feeling grateful that the cold weather earlier in the week had given way to a mild dampness, so that the grave-diggers had not been too hampered in their task.

On Guy's left he was aware of Claud, visibly moved, but standing stiffly to attention as befitted an ex-army officer; while Gertrude, on his other side, stared straight ahead of her, showing no sign of emotion at all until, quite suddenly, at the end of the burial service, she stepped forward and dropped a sprig of rosemary from the rectory garden on to the lowered coffin.

Walking back to the rectory, again between brother and sister, Guy Hennessey thought what a strange woman this niece of his was. In keeping with Dr Forman, he had never understood her. She seemed to show none of the natural attributes of womanhood. There were none of the endearing feminine traits such as those displayed by his wife, no cosy helplessness which had always appealed to his masculinity. Gertrude was altogether too self-sufficient. There was, of course, no doubt that she had been a virtual godsend to his brother-in-law after his wife died so unexpectedly, within three days, when a carbuncle on her neck had turned to septicaemia. Guy had had nothing but admiration for the way Gertrude had taken on the reins, looking after her father and brother and Netherford Rectory. Claud could only have been about ten or eleven, he supposed. He realised now what a very different character he was, compared to his sister. Claud was mercurial, impressionable. Guy had been a little concerned the previous evening to discover that the boy appeared rather too fond of his drink. Guy imagined the war and his wound might have had an effect on someone so young and sensitive. But he hoped this tendency wouldn't interfere with the excellent position which he had obtained for him and wondered whether he might have a quiet word with Gertrude about it, if he got the chance.

He was relieved when she herself made it unnecessary, by bringing up the future after the other overnight guests had departed the following day. He was staying on to lunch prior to catching an early afternoon train back to Laverton Hall.

"Claud and I have been discussing, Guy," she began — Gertrude had never prefaced his name with 'Uncle', something he had been forced to accept — "the possibility of setting up home together. I would be more than happy to take care of his domestic arrangements pending, of course, the time when he wants to marry. He seems to approve the idea." She shot a keen glance at her brother, who shuffled his feet and smiled, as if somewhat embarrassed. "I believe you told me about the various official residences given to the Palace staff in Lower Grosvenor Place," she went on, by no means embarrassed herself. "Do you think it might be possible for Claud to obtain one, providing his sister ran it? I think," she added, with a slightly quizzical smile, "I have the right credentials."

Sir Guy Hennessey was surprised, but quick to grasp the obvious advantages of such a situation. "Why, yes," he replied, slowly. "I can see it might be an excellent idea." Gertrude's chaperonage was just what the boy needed. Keep him on the straight and narrow. Guy knew exactly whom he could approach about the matter. Of course, it would probably have to be one of the smaller houses or apartments, but he would drop a hint in the right quarter. According to the will which had been read out by the family solicitor the previous evening, brother and sister had both been adequately provided for. The rector of Netherford had obviously decided that Gertrude was unlikely to marry and therefore a greater share of the residual estate had been allocated to her. Had his brother-in-law, Guy wondered, also been conscious that his son was not of the same calibre as his sister, and therefore a clause had been inserted to the effect that Claud could not inherit any of the capital outright until the age of twenty-five. That seemed highly likely. The Reverend George Kimberley had been a saintly man, but no fool. Yes, Guy thought, warming to Gertrude's idea of looking after Claud, she was no fool either. He would certainly do what he could.

As he settled himself into a first class carriage that afternoon in a train which stopped at Netherford Halt, he was already envisaging dinner at his

London club, putting the right word in the right ear, mentioning casually that the Bishop of Castlebury had conducted his brother-in-law's funeral, how splendidly everything had been managed by his niece, Miss Gertrude Kimberley, an asset to any establishment. Not a detail had been overlooked. He recalled how there was even a tin of his favourite biscuits, Bath Olivers, placed by his bed.

His thoughts turned to the rectory staff. All the meals had been quite excellent. That Charlotte Russe last night, for instance, was the best he had ever tasted. Gertrude would still require the services of domestics, whatever accommodation she might move into, but he doubted her cook would want to go to London. Somehow, he couldn't see Ethel Henstridge anywhere other than in the country. She must still have several more useful years ahead of her. He was glad he had left the woman a sizeable tip. He wondered whether she might be persuaded to come to Laverton Hall. Lilly, dear as she was, had never had Gertrude's knack of getting the best out of servants. Of course, his wife had other, more endearing qualities.

Especially when she was younger, before the arthritis set in. He smiled when he thought of them. Then, still scheming, he closed his eyes. Soon, he was asleep.

Oddly enough, the question of staff became the topic of conversation between Gertrude and Claud as they walked up to Castlebury Rings after seeing Guy off. "A lot will depend on where I move," Gertrude said, "but I have a strong feeling that Guy will pull off the London plan. He seemed most enthusiastic, didn't he? I believe he misses being at the top, not having a hand in things. He's still pretty influential. I should think we might easily hear before long. And the staff will want to know. I dare say Ethel will wish to stay at the rectory with the new incumbent. I should think whoever it is would jump at the chance of taking her on. I'll have to have a cook in London, of course, but I can't see Ethel coming with me. She's part and parcel of the village. So is Shiner. And I'm sure Dyer's mother will want to keep an eye on him."

"What about the tweenies?"

"Oh, Guy. You shouldn't call them that. They're house-parlourmaids. Dora is coming along splendidly. She's more intelligent than Gladys. In fact, wherever I go, I feel I should like to take Dora with me. I've gone to a lot of trouble training her and I must say it's been very rewarding. She's polite and willing and she's used to my ways."

For a moment, Claud wondered what Gertrude's ways were, what it was like working for his sister. He wouldn't care for it himself, but he had no doubt she was fair, if incredibly firm.

"I'm sure the Pennys wouldn't mind," went on Gertrude. "They'd know Dora would be safe with me."

Claud took a sideways glance at his sister. Yes, he supposed people would feel safe with Gertie. In a way, he himself did. She had always been there, in the background, comforting him when he had fallen out of a willow tree by the stream which ran through the rectory garden, superintending the packing of his trunk when he went off to preparatory school after nannie left, and then seeing he had all the right uniform and equipment for Harrow. He recalled how she used to arrive there with his father on certain occasions, invariably reserved and unobtrusively dressed. She had always seemed older than her age, but he remembered how shocked he had been when a boy called Jackson asked if she was his mother. Jackson had invited him to stay shortly before they both joined up. He had fallen violently in love with his sister. Alicia was quite beautiful. She hadn't taken any notice of him, of course. She had been too busy flirting with an army captain home on leave. He had watched her, covertly, pictured them kissing when they suddenly seemed to disappear from the others around the tennis court. He wished he had not accepted his friend's invitation. The days were bad enough, the nights pure torture.

After he had 'got over' Alicia, he had become quite taken with Sidney Forman's only daughter, Connie. She had none of Alicia's allure but, at seventeen, she was turning into quite an attractive girl in a pleasant, pink and plumpish sort of way. He had written to her from the front but, when London claimed him after his discharge he had forgotten all about her in the new and exciting life he was leading. Now, he felt a twinge of guilt that he had never answered her last letter. Casually, he asked Gertrude what she was doing and was not altogether surprised when she answered, "Connie's taken up nursing, Claud. She's a probationer in Castlebury General Infirmary. She was very cut up when Henry was killed just before the armistice. So was the whole family. I doubt Mrs Forman will ever get over it. Nor Sidney, for that matter. I'm thankful they've still got Reginald. He wasn't allowed to break off his doctor's training at Barts during the war. He's a fully-fledged GP now, married and doing quite well, I believe, with a practice in the home counties."

Claud thought of Reginald, a dark, saturnine, enigmatic sort of individual. A little like Gertrude, in a way.

"You and he were quite close, weren't you," he remarked, "once upon a time?"

She looked at him, sharply. "What makes you say that?"

"I thought you used to come up here together sometimes. Looking for witches, especially on Hallowe'en night. I once overheard Shiner telling Fred Penny about it."

"What a ridiculous notion. I thought I'd taught you never to listen to servants' gossip."

Gertrude strode on ahead. He was surprised she seemed so rattled. He felt he had made a perfectly harmless observation. A lot of young people did that sort of thing. He remembered being sorry that he hadn't been considered old enough to accompany them. After all, it was only a bit of fun — except that he could not quite connect Gertie with fun.

4

GERTRUDE and Claud Kimberley moved into the Wenhams' former home in Lower Grosvenor Place in the late summer of 1919. Both were surprised that they had been allocated quite such a large establishment; but it would seem that their uncle had more than come up to expectations in acting on their behalf. Well versed in the old boy network, Sir Guy Hennessey had pulled all the right strings and had done all the necessary entertaining, both at his London club and Laverton Hall. He privately regretted that the meals at the latter were nothing compared to those with which he had been regaled at Netherford Rectory but Lilly, his wife, had played her part admirably as the appealing, slightly coquettish, hostess — in spite of her arthritic condition — and had backed him up whenever he had mentioned Gertrude's extreme competence and

35

Claud's immense charm and diplomacy. (Guy had completely persuaded himself that his nephew's tendency towards intemperance was only slight and would soon be taken care of by his astute sister.)

There was only one stipulation in connection with the pair taking up residence at Number 20, and that was to do with the top floor. The authorities wished this to be temporarily kept available for any bachelor who might possibly be returning from a diplomatic mission abroad and awaiting a new posting in England. Gertrude readily agreed to this. The house had a large basement area as well as a roomy fourth floor, capable of providing sleeping quarters for any domestics she chose to employ. As she had already anticipated, Ethel Henstridge did not want to leave Netherford and although Gertrude, as a token of gratitude towards her uncle, had done her best to persuade her cook to go to Laverton Hall, Ethel had remained determined to stay on her home ground and was only too pleased to be taken on by the new incumbents at the rectory, the Reverend and Mrs Pemberton.

As the Wenhams were taking their own cook with them to Hampton Court, Gertrude had travelled to London and stayed at a hotel where, sent by one of the top domestic agencies, she had interviewed several women for the post of cook/housekeeper, even though she herself was determined to keep as tight a rein on the establishment as possible. At the same time, she also arranged to employ the Wenhams' daily kitchen maid, a weekly washerwoman and one living-in house-parlourmaid, explaining that she was hoping to bring another one up with her from Netherford.

Dora Penny was excited beyond measure at the prospect of living in London, although she had at first been afraid that opposition, particularly from her father, would prevent it. When she had visited her parents on her half day off just after Gertrude had been down to their cottage to put forward her proposition, Dora could not understand why her father seemed so much more against the idea than her mother. She would have been even more mystified had she heard some of the troubled conversations which went on between man and wife for another week, after which time they had promised to give Gertrude their answer.

Each evening they had sat up in the small cramped and only living-room, the firelight from the cooking range flickering on their worn anxious faces, as they discussed the pros and cons of letting their youngest — and prettiest — daughter move so far away from home into a big city, and a capital one at that.

On the last night before Gertrude was due to call again, Edith Penny, who was always keen for her children to do as well as possible, said, "The girl wants to go, Fred. And it isn't as if she won't be well looked after. Miss Gertrude's strict but she's fair. I'd sooner our Dora worked for her than someone we don't know nothing about. Besides, Miss Gertrude seems to have taken to her and Dora's been happy at the rectory since she left school."

"Yes, but we don't know as how she'll be happy in London, do we? And where will she go on her half day?"

Question and answer went back and forth, the man still fearful, the woman torn between maternal protective love and the desire for a daughter's betterment.

"Miss Gertrude says as how she's engaged another house-parlourmaid. I dare say they could go out with each other."

"Don't talk daft, Edie. When one maid's out, t'other would have to be in."

Edith Penny realised her remark was not exactly clever. Presently, she said, "I could write to Cousin Fanny."

"But she'm nowhere near where the King lives, Edie." Even Fred, who had never been further than twenty miles from Netherford in his life, knew that Cousin Fanny's home in somewhere called Tooting Bec would hardly likely to be close to Buckingham Palace. Moreover, they had almost lost touch with Fanny since she left Netherford a long time ago.

An uneasy silence fell between them. Fred wondered whether to mention the Castlebury Rings affair. Of course, it was way back before the war. He had never liked to say anything about it, even to his wife. Edie might talk. As a loyal employee of the doctor he had decided that, except for Shiner, the least said soonest mended. Besides, Miss Gertrude had been a lot younger then. She was now a highly respected, early middle-aged inhabitant of Netherford, looked up to by all and sundry.

Yet Fred Penny had never forgotten the evening when he and Dr Forman had been called up by Jim Butt, the local gamekeeper on the Netherford estate. It had been Hallowe'en night and Jim had come running down from his cottage on the downs saying his wife was in labour and the midwife, Mother Barnes, needed help. Fred had got out the pony and trap and driven Jim and the doctor back up towards Castlebury Rings as fast as he could get Punch, his employer's fat cob, to travel. For the weather had been terrible, the wind sweeping down over the valley and icy needles of rain seeming to come sideways, drenching the three occupants of the trap. On the way they had passed a man and a woman walking towards the village, but it was too dark and their mission too hazardous and urgent for the three men to take much notice of them, even if they could have seen their faces.

It was only many hours later, when Dr Forman had performed a near miracle on a breech birth and delivered Jim's wife of a bouncing eight pound baby boy and Fred himself was tucked up in bed warming himself against Edith's comforting body and the stone hot water bottle she had placed at his feet, that he had started to think how strange it was that any two people had been out and about on such a night, presumably returning from the downs.

Being a taciturn man, he had never said anything about the incident to anyone until, some years later, after Jim Butt had lost his job on the Netherford estate — it had been rumoured that a number of pheasants brought down by his lordship's guns did not always find their demise recorded in the game book — that Fred had happened to meet the disgraced gamekeeper, who had somehow managed to obtain another post a little further afield. They had met in a local inn while Fred was waiting for Dr Forman and his wife, who were visiting friends. Fred had enquired after the baby which had been born on what he referred to as 'the worst night in Christendom', and had been pleased to hear that the child was doing well.

"I've often thought," Fred went on, "how odd it was to have seen that couple we passed on the way up to your cottage. I mean, 'tweren't exactly courting weather, were it? You may not have noticed 'em."

Jim had then given one of his knowing smiles. "Oh, I saw 'em all right, Didn'st thee know who 'twere?"

"No."

"That were the rector's daughter and Master Reginald, the doctor's son. They often used to carry on up there at Castlebury Rings."

"Carry on?" Fred frowned. "On a night like that?"

"Well, I don't reckon as how they was doing the usual sort of carry-on that night. But they were a pair and no mistake. God knows what they did get

42

up to sometimes. 'Specially Hallowe'en. It's my belief that Gertie fancied she was a bit of a witch. 'Course, summer nights, they could well have gone in for another kind of caper. Although I never caught 'em at it."

Fred had been shocked. It was then that he had spoken to Shiner about what Jim had told him. After all, they were both employed by the fathers of the offspring in question. He had hoped that Jim was lying. He wouldn't put it past him. Fred had been disappointed when Shiner had replied, cheerfully. "Well, I've allus known as how Miss Gertrude was sweet on Master Reggie when she was young. 'Course, it's all over now, him bein' married and all that. I dunno how much there were in it. But I knows both of 'em were fond of the Rings. Dancin' about they was, Jim once told I. Must 'ave been just arter the war started because Miss Gertie was wearing that cloak o' hers. Come to think of it, top it wi' a tall hat and you could almost see her on a broomstick."

Fred had never repeated their conversation and he did not mention it to Edith now.

He could see how set she seemed to have become on Dora bettering herself, as she put it. Besides, whatever Miss Gertie had got up to with the doctor's son was such a long, a very long time ago.

5

WHY *do I love you? Why do you love me?* sang out Claud Kimberley's gramophone in the New Year of 1920.

Gertrude, doing her best to be tolerant, closed the door of the little mezzanine room she had adapted as a study for herself between the first and second floors at Lower Grosvenor Place. Even so, she was still uncomfortably aware of *I'll be loving you, always* now coming from her brother's bedroom and infiltrating the various levels of their new home.

Dora Penny, undressing on the fourth floor in the room she shared with Nellie Giffin, the other house-parlourmaid, said to her room mate, "Reckon she wot gets Mr Claud for a 'usband will be a lucky girl."

Nellie, brought up in the east end of London and a great deal more knowing and mature for her age than Dora, asked, "Wot makes you say that?"

"Him's so romantic, Nellie," replied Dora. She had heard the word from Ethel Henstridge back in Netherford, although she had only lately come to appreciate its full meaning. To Dora, Claud Kimberley was the most wonderful, handsomest and cleverest young man in the whole world. And when she sometimes answered the door to an elegant young lady who was prepared to brave Gertrude's hawk-eyed chaperonage, Dora would go to bed dreaming of a wedding soon to follow, with Mr Claud, a wounded hero from the war, waiting for his bride at the altar, his tall distinguished figure turning just in time to greet a vision in white satin and lace, walking slowly up the aisle of some church, possibly rather larger than the one she had known all her life in Netherford.

Dora's dreams — and sometimes daydreams — never included herself. She merely worshipped Mr Claud from afar. He was, in her simple innocent mind, a godlike being, remote, already bespoke to some female creature who lived in a different world. It was a world which was quite apart from her own, one which involved men wearing white tie and tails, pretty ladies with bobbed hair wearing gorgeous ball gowns, or going to the theatre in daringly short-skirted silk creations, topped with white fur jackets. It was a world of endless excitements — and risks. There were drinks called cocktails which Dora, much to her dismay, had overheard Miss Gertrude telling her brother she would never serve at Number 20. There were motorcars such as Mr Claud's, something else about which Miss Gertrude disapproved and had told him off for driving too fast. When he was subsequently fined for exceeding the official speed limit of twenty miles per hour along Piccadilly, Dora's heart had gone out to him.

She was not in the slightest bit jealous or envious of all the goings-on in which she had no part. That was not her nature. The difference between the world of her employers and herself was simply a fact of life. Dora merely felt more than lucky to find herself working so close to the King of England's home for a good mistress — even if she was a bit of a tartar — and a perfect young master for whom she thought she would have done anything.

A few weeks after Dora's chance remark to her room mate about Claud's seeming perfection, the two young girls were again getting ready for bed, when Nellie suddenly said, "If I was you, my girl, I'd watch it. You're soft on Mr Claud, aren't you?" Dora, her head just emerging from the neck of her nightgown, stared at Nellie in amazement.

"Of course not. How could I be?" she had replied. "Mr Claud's Miss Gertrude's brother, the rector of Netherford's only son."

"So?" Nellie Giffin, already running to fat, unhooked her stays with which her mother had provided her, took off her woollen combinations, pulled on her own flannelette nightgown and clambered on to the iron bedstead, the hard metal springs creaking under her weight. "I only said, Dora," she went on, as she settled herself down to sleep, "Thee's best watch it. Or watch Mr Claud, more likely."

"*Watch Mr Claud*?" Dora was completely mystified. "Why should I watch 'im, Nellie?"

"I've seen 'im looking at you, Dora. He fancies a bit o' skirt."

"Fancies a bit o' skirt?"

"Oh, come off it," came the reply from under the bedclothes. "Surely thee knows what men wants. All men."

Dora, shivering, slid quickly into her own bed. "No, I don't know, Nellie. Wot do 'em want?"

"To put their dicks into a woman's cunt, if they get the chance."

Dora had never heard the words 'cunt' or 'dick'. For all the poverty and privations of her upbringing, the Pennys had been good parents who had never used bad language in front of their children. Yet now, albeit vaguely, came the realisation of what Nellie was trying to tell her and, at the same time, a certain hitherto unknown thrill. She was glad when snores put an end to Nellie's loose talk, as she herself lay awake a long time thinking about their conversation.

When Dora eventually slept, her dreams were frightening and confused. Claud Kimberley was somehow approaching her, bending over her, telling her how pretty she was, how he would take care of her, how he wanted . . . And here, the dream stopped suddenly. She woke, shouting, enough to wake Nellie also. Without being exactly aware of it, the latter, in the crudest way, had jolted Dora into a maturity for which she was singularly unprepared.

To her relief, in the weeks that followed, Nellie did not bring up the subject again, possibly sensing how much she had upset her friend. And, indeed, Dora found herself increasingly nervous in Claud's presence. It was as if something — she knew not what — had been spoiled.

One afternoon in March, she happened to be alone in Number 20. Gertrude was out — she went out quite a lot now, although the staff never knew exactly where — and it was Nellie's half day off. The daily kitchenmaid was sick and Ada Bagwell, the cook/housekeeper, had told Dora that she wanted to meet her soldier brother at Victoria station on his way up north, so that she wouldn't be back until four thirty. Dora was fairly sure that Ada had not mentioned this to

Miss Gertrude, because it was one of her employer's rules that there must always be two domestics in the house at the same time. But, naturally, she had said nothing while Ada Bagwell instructed her to make up the bed in the top floor flat while she was out, as they were expecting a temporary visitor from overseas that night. Ada also stressed that she must listen out for the doorbell.

Dora found herself actually rather pleased to be left in charge, although she wasn't too happy about Miss Gertrude's orders being broken. It was when she was carrying up some fresh linen from the laundry room that she heard the front door slam and, leaning over the banisters, she saw Claud Kimberley bounding up the stairs two at a time. Overtaking her on the landing outside his bedroom, he smiled and said, "Why, hello Dora. How quiet it is. Is everyone out?"

"Yes, sir."

"Ah. I see."

He looked at her speculatively. She expected him to go straight to his room. Instead, he paused a moment, saw what she was carrying and remarked, "You

51

must be preparing for our new guest."

"Yes, sir."

"Let me carry all that for you."

Dora was horrified. "Oh no, sir. Thank you all the same, sir. It's no trouble."

"Nothing's ever too much trouble for you, is it, Dora?" he said, as he more or less forced her into handing over the bedding to him.

She was devastated, as he went ahead of her up to the top floor. He was acting so strangely, so out of keeping. She was sure Miss Gertrude wouldn't approve of her allowing him to help. Nor would Ada Bagwell. It was now two p.m. She was thankful that neither would be returning until at least four thirty.

It seemed that Mr Claud was also considering how long it would be before any member of the household returned for, as he laid down the clean sheets and pillow-cases on the bed in the top floor, he suddenly remarked, "So they've left you to hold the fort, have they, Dora?"

"The fort, sir?"

Claud laughed out loud. "Well, yes.

Just an expression for someone who's been asked to take care of everything alone."

She gave a small smile. "Just until half past four, sir."

"How fortuitous."

She had no idea what the word meant. She supposed he was still on about forts. Then she heard him enquire, "Why don't you and I hear a little music? You like my records, don't you, Dora? I've got a new jazz one. Let's go down and listen to it."

She was mesmerised. Mr Claud was *actually asking* her to come down and listen to his gramophone. Yet, much as she admired him, she knew that he was suggesting something wrong. Didn't he realise it himself? Apparently not. Or surely he wouldn't have asked her? Perhaps if she just went for a little while ... It wouldn't hurt, would it? No one would know. Then she would excuse herself by saying that she had to prepare for their visitor.

Dora was surprised when, once in Mr Claud's bedroom, he did not go over to his gramophone straight away and put on the jazz record. Instead, he closed the door and locked it. Then, standing facing her with his back against it, he said, "Did anyone ever tell you, Dora, that you're devilish pretty. Enough to drive a man mad."

The colour swept to her face. She stared at him, remembering Nellie's warning. Her heart was pounding as he came over to where she was standing. As he caught hold of her with both arms she let out a small strangled, "Please, sir," to which he replied, again laughing, "I think we could just forget about the 'sir' for this afternoon, don't you, Dora?"

Afterwards, she could never exactly remember how it was that she found herself on the bed, struggling as Claud Kimberley pulled and tugged at her underwear, while calling her "a little vixen", "a tease", "a hussy" and accusing her of lately having tried to lead him on by purposely avoiding him.

When, eventually, he entered her, she cried out in pain and remained cowed and whimpering until, minutes later, he rolled off her saying, "My God, Dora. I never expected a sumsie wench like you to be a virgin. This bed's in a hell of a mess. I think you'd better get some clean sheets and remake it, as well as the one in the top flat."

6

IT was the laundry which created suspicion in Gertrude's mind, at first centred on the honesty or, rather, dishonesty, of Mrs Prinn, the washerwoman.

She was an unprepossessing scrawny individual with a permanently dripping nose and rough, reddened hands through long years of working at her hard dreary task. She had, however, been recommended by the Wenhams and, so far, had meticulously entered in a little book all the items she had washed on Mondays and returned to iron on Wednesdays. This was checked by Ada Bagwell, who then submitted it to her employer on Fridays, along with various other household bills.

Until now, Mrs Prinn had never laundered more than four linen hemstitched sheets each week for Gertrude's and Claud's beds, unless they had a visitor in the top flat when there were six. Members of the domestic staff had to make do with calico ones and were issued with a single, usually sides-to-middle sheet every Monday, only the bottom one being sent to the laundry. After the week of Dora's deflowering, Mrs Prinn found herself washing eight of the best.

Gertrude, puzzling over the sudden increase, rang the bell from her study and told a white-faced Dora that she wished to speak to Mrs Bagwell.

"Can you account for the extra number of hemstitched sheets washed last Monday?" she enquired, as soon as the cook/housekeeper entered the room.

"Why, no, madam. I was surprised myself." Ada Bagwell had been afraid she had been summoned to the mezzanine room because her employer had somehow discovered that she had slipped out for an unauthorised afternoon off the previous week. She was relieved when it was merely laundry which seemed to be exercising Miss Gertrude's mind.

"Our guest was only here a couple of nights, Mrs Bagwell," Gertrude went on. "There was no reason to change either

Mr Claud's or my sheets more than once, was there?"

"Oh, no, madam."

"Have you checked that there are the right number of clean sheets in the airing cupboard?"

"Yes, madam."

Gertrude frowned. "When Mrs Prinn comes next Monday, please tell her I want to see her."

"Yes, madam."

Gertrude did not like to feel that something was going on which she did not understand. She puzzled over the question of the extra laundry more than once during the weekend. She was also concerned that the Penny girl did not look well. There were dark rings under her eyes and her usually obliging manner seemed to have given way to a kind of abject lassitude. Although Gertrude had only seen the lighter side of nursing in the war, nevertheless she was always quick to detect any signs of illness in her staff. After all, a sick servant was an inefficient one. She wondered whether uprooting Dora from the country had been altogether wise.

Dora herself was now wishing devoutly she had never left Netherford. She felt wretched in mind and body. After Claud had left her that fateful afternoon, she had succeeded — although only just — in pulling herself together enough to change both sheets on his bed, carefully sponging out as far as possible any telltale patches of red before putting them in the dirty linen basket. She had then managed to complete her duties in the top flat before Ada Bagwell's return. But she did not know how she would be able to continue to carry them out when in the presence of Claud Kimberley again. That night, she thanked God that both her employers had gone, with their new guest, to some reception.

In the days that followed, Dora could not understand how it was that Claud Kimberley appeared to be so completely at ease, as if nothing had taken place between them. When she was obliged to wait at table, she heard him talking to his sister in his usual lighthearted bantering manner. In fact, if anything, he seemed more cheerful and self-confident than ever, as he discussed some play he had seen in the company of several other young people to whom Dora had previously opened the front door.

But the most difficult and hardest part of her ordeal was trying to hide what had happened from Nellie Giffin. Sharp, cynical and nosy, Nellie was soon aware that something had gone very wrong for Dora. Having been out on the afternoon which had changed her friend's life, she had no means of knowing that Dora had been alone in the house before Claud had come back so unexpectedly. Yet it was plain to her that the young master — as Ada Bagwell referred to him — must have somehow made a pass at her friend, as she herself had foreseen might happen. That Dora had taken it so hardly genuinely distressed her for, though tough and seemingly unsympathetic, she wished sincerely she could do something to help. That things had gone so totally out of control and that Dora had been not only seduced but virtually raped was something, naturally, she would never have envisaged.

Until, after a few weeks, the sickness started. One morning, when Dora was too ill to stagger downstairs to start work at six thirty a.m., Nellie, horrified, stared at her, saying, "Thee can't be . . You're not . . . " simply to be answered by floods of tears. Although Dora had been so abysmally ignorant of sex and had never before thought about what took place, she was aware that the cessation of a woman's periods usually meant she was pregnant.

Gertrude, told of the girl's indisposition after breakfast, asked that she should be sent to her as soon as she was dressed. At ten o'clock, an exceedingly washed-out and terrified young house-parlourmaid presented herself in the mezzanine room.

"Close the door, Dora, and sit down."

After the girl had done as she was bidden, Gertrude looked at her for a few moments without speaking. Her dark piercing eyes seemed to travel all over the small frame, taking in everything. As a rector's daughter, she had seen enough of the 'fallen' back in Netherford. It had often been her unenviable task to visit the home of someone who was 'in the family way'. She could see now, at

61

a glance, that Dora was pregnant. But where . . . how . . . ? The Penny girl had been dutiful and trustworthy in the extreme. On her half days off she had once gone Christmas shopping but at other times she had managed to make her way to Tooting Bec on a bus, where she had relations. According to Ada Bagwell, a woman called Fanny Grice always escorted her back to Lower Grosvenor Place by nine o'clock sharp. In fact, if either house-parlourmaid was likely to give trouble, Gertrude thought it might have been Nellie, a coarser and less respectful character altogether.

Coming straight to the point, Gertrude said, "I understand you have been sick, Dora."

"Yes, ma'am." The eyes in the white face seemed enormous.

"Do you know why?"

There was silence, a silence of confirmation.

"On your half days off, Dora, have you been seeing some young man?"

"No, ma'am."

"But it is possible, is it not, that you might be pregnant?"

Again there was an ominous silence, more meaningful than any verbal answer.

"In fact, you know you are pregnant?" Gertrude persisted.

The terrified eyes looked down at the floor.

"You realise, Dora, that I shall have to send you home? Write to your parents."

"Yes, ma'am." The voice was merely a whisper now.

"Who is the father of the child you are expecting, Dora?"

It seemed, in the long silence that followed, that the ticking of Gertrude's carriage clock on the mantelpiece became actually louder, until drowned by Dora's sobs.

Then the ghastly truth suddenly dawned on Gertrude. Could it be? Yes, it must. Those extra sheets . . . There had never been a satisfactory answer. Somehow at some time, Gertrude knew not when, Claud and Dora must have been alone in his bedroom. She thought she had been so careful to insist that there must always be two domestics on duty in the house at the same time. But apparently this order had been flouted.

Swiftly, she changed tactics. She did not need, nor did she wish, to drag any further revelations or confessions out of Dora Penny. She knew enough. It would be better if the whole situation were quickly hushed up. Even if Claud guessed, he was still just under age, wasn't he? Need he, in fact, ever be told exactly why Dora had been sent home at once. She could be said to be suffering from anaemia, too delicate for London. She, Gertrude, would write to the Pennys. She would accept full responsibility because their daughter was so young and still under her care. Hopefully, Dora's parents could be bought, as well as their silence. There would have to be maintenance. She would go to a solicitor. Get some kind of agreement drawn up. Presumably she and the girl's father would have to sign something. But, after all, it was the sort of thing which often happened, didn't it? She seemed to recall it being put about that Shiner's wife was the daughter of an earl, something about a top hat which her mother had always kept in a cupboard. If there was talk between the servants at Number 20, that was just too bad.

But if neither Dora nor Claud admitted anything, nothing could be proved. The sooner she got the girl out of the house, the better.

Thank God, Gertrude thought, that Claud had just been invited to spend some leave with his uncle and aunt.

7

AS was only to be expected, Edith and Fred Penny took the news of Dora's impending return with dismay and bewilderment.

The very next day after their daughter's distressing interview with her employer, they received a letter from Gertrude saying that, owing to unfortunate and unforeseen circumstances, she was arranging for Dora to be put on a train the following morning which would be arriving at Netherford Halt at two thirty p.m. Perhaps Mr or Mrs Penny would meet it? She said that she would be writing more fully as soon as possible which, while naturally making no mention of the fact, would be after she had been to see her solicitor.

Fred and Edith had just finished their breakfast of bread and dripping washed down with strong tea, when Gertrude's missive arrived.

"She's got the sack," Edith cried, rocking backwards and forwards in her chair by the range, the letter — which had taken her and Fred a little while to decipher — still clutched in her hand.

Fred, slower and less voluble than his wife, replied, "We don't know as yet, Edie. Maybe the girl's ill."

"But Miss Gertrude would 'ave said. It's the sack, I tell 'e. Thee mark my words. 'Twill be all over Netherford. What can the maid 'ave done? Dora was allus such a good girl. Can thee meet 'er wi' the trap? She'll no doubt have her box." Never for one moment did Edith Penny entertain the idea of a possible pregnancy.

"I'll ask Doctor. I dare say as how 'twill be all right. Don't 'e fret, Edie."

To his credit, Fred did not repeat the doubts he had always had in the first place about the wisdom of letting Dora go to London. Now, although he did his best to comfort his wife, he was gripped by fear as he went out to get Punch and the trap ready for the morning rounds. It was not quite the same kind of fear as when he had heard that two of his sons were off to the front, nor when he saw Dickie Musselwhite, the telegraph boy, coming to the door with the dreaded orange envelope in his hand which Fred had opened to learn that one of his sons had been killed on the Somme. Those had been terrible times; but this present fear was somehow greater because it was more nebulous and seemed to be connected with shame. Dora had always been his favourite child. He knew that there was something wrong, very wrong. In his day he'd seen enough young women suddenly sent home from service and it was nearly all for the same reason. Many was the time he'd subsequently had to wait outside some cottage while the doctor was attending a birth, often a difficult one, like when Jim Butt's wife was nigh at death's door. Only on that occasion the woman in question had at least been married. Fred could think of a lot of others when Dr Forman had brought a bastard into the world.

During the morning, sitting in the trap outside the various homes of his employer's patients, Fred had plenty of time to reflect still further. If, as he feared, his daughter was pregnant, who was the scoundrel who had taken advantage of her? That she would have been an innocent victim he had no doubt. He felt he would have cheerfully killed any man who had laid a hand on her. Somehow he did not think she had met up with a stranger. Fanny Grice, who had been surprisingly helpful considering they had had so little contact, seemed to have been most conscientious in escorting Dora back to Lower Grosvenor Place on her half days off. Although, cynically, Fred could not help wondering whether having a young relation working in such close proximity to Buckingham Palace — for a member of its distinguished staff, at that — might have had something to do with it. Nevertheless, it had been a comfort to him and Edith to know how well their youngest daughter was being taken care of. Since Dora had left Netherford the previous year, her letters, though written in an immature and ungrammatical way, had all been happy ones. This had done much to back up Edith's cautious approval of the arrangement and to dispel Fred's misgivings.

Yet, now, Dora was being sent home due to 'unfortunate and unforeseen circumstances'. The words kept repeating themselves in his brain. When, the morning rounds over, he helped the doctor out of his trap and asked, haltingly, whether he could use it to meet her at two thirty the next day at Netherford Halt, the good man looked at him in some surprise.

"Dora? Coming home? Good gracious. Is it a holiday already? She's not been gone a year, surely?"

"No, zur." Fred's voice was gruff. Then, looking his employer straight in the face, he continued, "The missus and I 'ave only just heard. We don't rightly know why she's bein' sent 'ome."

Dr Forman was getting on in years. He was a well-qualified, highly respected and dedicated general practitioner; but he had always felt that he had remained a student so far as human nature was concerned. Even now, he was still learning. The only thing he knew for sure was that nothing surprised him. He thought of the Penny family. There wasn't a better nor more upright one in the whole district. He had brought Dora into the world. He remembered how badly Edith had gone down after the birth with puerperal fever. There had been five other children before Dora. He had done all he could to help. He realised that Fred's wife was worn out. He had watched her battle against depression for many months. He could not but admire the way she had fought through it, had done her best to see that none of her family suffered, especially the last of her brood who, thank God, had grown into a healthy sturdy child and, with puberty, showed all the makings of becoming a beauty. He knew how Edith and Fred had felt about letting her go to London, how Edith had been keen for the girl to do well for herself, how Fred was possibly more aware of the dangers of a wider world into which he had never actually stepped.

Sidney Forman could recall how he himself had last seen Dora, smiling and waving goodbye from the trap when her father had driven her to Netherford Halt. It had been harvest time. They were stooking oats on the Netherford estate. The countryside had been humming with activity. The air was warm and sweet-scented. There had been much to look forward to. The war was over. There were no more telegrams from the War Office such as the ones which told both him and Fred that one of their sons had been killed. One never got over a thing like that, but he knew life had to go on and, on the day Dora left for London, although he was not as religious a man as his friend, the late rector, he had found himself sending up a little prayer that her obvious happiness would be maintained.

Having told Fred to take the trap next day by all means, they went to their respective homes, preoccupied and troubled. Had they known it, both men were trying to reject the same thought: that while they had a grudging respect for Gertrude, they had no such feelings for her brother. The doctor was well aware that Claud was a weak character, which his sister's obsessive mothering had done nothing to improve. Sidney Forman had never told the boy's father, but after Claud had been discharged from the army some papers had been sent to him from the medical authorities, the gist of them being that a more seasoned officer would have taken his wound with greater fortitude and been likely to have recovered more quickly. Reading between the lines, Sidney Forman knew that Claud had obviously not shone as an officer and, with the war drawing to an end, the army was glad to be shot of him.

Fred, with no such knowledge or powers of deduction as his employer, nevertheless also knew that Claud Kimberley was 'a wrong 'un'. But a loyal unwritten code of conduct forbade him to voice this feeling to anyone, least of all his wife. After he had so stoically said goodbye to Dora at Netherford Halt, he had tried to console himself with the thought that Gertrude would see she came to no harm, in the same way as she would keep a vigilant eye on her brother.

Yet, as he and Edith lay awake that night, both wondering what the morrow would bring, Fred couldn't help also thinking that Gertrude, for all her outward semblance of strict propriety, was not an altogether straightforward character. He had never forgotten what Jim Butt had told him about the goings-on at Castlebury Rings.

8

GERTRUDE decided not to use the same solicitors who had helped her with the various negotiations concerning taking over the tenancy of Number 20, Lower Grosvenor Place. They were too closely associated with the Palace. Instead, she chose an obscure firm off the Caledonian Road, whose name she had been given by the 'consultant' she saw in Wimpole Street every Tuesday.

She had never told anyone about these weekly visits. She was aware that she was doing something unorthodox, which might be frowned on by certain members of the Establishment and incomprehensible to the more ordinary members of society. She supposed, in some way, she was indulging herself, dabbling in the occult. Even as a child, she had been interested in it. She had never quite accepted the Christian faith in which she had been brought up. Every Sunday she had watched her father conduct matins in Netherford church and, later, after she was confirmed, had knelt to accept communion from him.

But, later still, when he had asked her to "draw near with faith" she had wanted to ask, "What sign have you had? Why is Mrs Stamp up at Netherford Lodge screaming with pain? How do you account for Bill Wetherby, the thatcher, falling off his ladder and leaving a widow and seven children?"

But she hadn't liked to. She had known her father was a good, a *really* good man, and the better side of Gertrude did not want to make it difficult for him. She could think of many a text he used for a sermon, especially the one about doubting Thomas: *blessed are they that have not seen and yet have believed.* As for her mother, Gertrude had always felt that to express any lack of faith to her would be equally unthinkable. She was too remote and devout, too wrapped up in her husband and his calling. After Mrs Kimberley died, so tragically and unexpectedly, Gertrude had been even more determined to seek some other solution to her problems.

When she began seeing more of Reginald Forman just before the war, she realised she had found a kindred spirit. He was following in his father's footsteps although, whereas the elder man never questioned Christianity, Reginald, starting his medical training at Barts and witnessing the poverty and appalling overcrowding in the East End of London, was fast losing the altruism which had propelled him into medicine in the first place. On his visits home, he had found he had more in common with Gertrude Kimberley than any member of his own family. Together, they would discuss life and death and, although such nomenclature would scarcely have been used in those days, alternative religion and alternative medicine.

She found him attractive, in a brooding melancholy way. She liked his theories about power, particularly the power of healing, not necessarily through religion. She was fascinated by his knowledge of anatomy and his detailed description of his anatomical studies. She found the speculative way he looked at her while discussing such activities, somehow exciting.

One warm midsummer's night, they had walked up to Castlebury Rings and he had asked, in what seemed a perfectly natural way, whether he might examine her body because, unlike the others he had been obliged to study, hers seemed such a splendidly healthy one. She had readily acquiesced. She had undressed. He was very thorough and he had taken a long time. At the end, he had seduced her with an expertise to which she responded with an abandon which surprised them both. He assured her that he would never allow her to become pregnant and their relationship would simply remain a shared and closely-guarded secret.

Thereafter, whenever the opportunity arose which, owing to his studies and the weather, was not often, they would creep back to their original mating ground where, naked and unashamed, they would perform the same ritual: a lengthy examination followed by intercourse. Occasionally, in winter, they had copulated in some disused barn, but it was always in the open air at the Rings where Gertrude experienced her greatest thrill. She had been younger then and less severe-looking. He had called her his beautiful witch, his pagan patient.

She had missed him desperately whenever he returned to London and when, during the war, his visits to Netherford became less and less, she compensated for her frustration by throwing all her energies into her duties as a VAD and various good works around the village. She was flattered that many of the officers she came across at the convalescent home seemed to enjoy talking to her but, possibly because of his singular method of arousing her, Reginald remained the only man to whom she was physically attracted.

She was devastated when she heard that he had suddenly married a young nurse, even though, in some strange way, she had never really expected him to marry her. She realised that what they had in common was abnormal, that it had little to do with romance. She had wanted to learn more about sexual deviation and paganism, but there was naturally no one she could ask nor any book she could turn to.

It was not until she got to London that Gertrude began to think she might have the opportunity to delve a little deeper into the mysterious practices she had only been vaguely aware of in her youth. At one of the dinner parties she found herself attending with increasing frequency, the name of a Dr Coué from America was brought to her attention. His devotees called him Professor and his treatment of those who sought his help was through autosuggestion. Anyone who fancied him or herself sick was persuaded to chant, "Day by day and in every way I am getting better and better".

Although Gertrude enjoyed good health, nevertheless a cult such as this greatly attracted her. When a certain Lady Atherton spoke to her about an oriental, a disciple of Dr Coué, who went rather further — although in what way Cicely Atherton did not explain — Gertrude asked her, casually, for his name. Soon afterwards, she made an appointment with him.

She found 'Doctor' — as he styled himself — Shaffi charming and sympathetic.

He was a swarthy individual, in physique not unlike Reginald. After each Tuesday session she felt released. But it was by no means a one-way relationship. He was responsive, even though she lay on his couch and he sat behind her head so that she never actually saw him while she found herself talking, without restraint or self-consciousness, about her upbringing, her father, her scepticism and lack of faith, free love, surrealism and whether the saxophone was the voice of the devil. They also discussed the theories of Freud and Jung, Sir Arthur Conan Doyle, Sir Oliver Lodge, ouija boards and even sex-magic rites. After she got to know him better, she began describing her one and only love affair, which she had not actually felt to have had much to do with love.

"But the physical urge is the greatest force in the history of mankind," she remembered him saying, just before she learnt of Dora's downfall.

At a later session with Dr Shaffi, Gertrude had been unable to refrain from telling him all about this: her initial shock, her sudden suspicion confirmed by the alteration in the laundry list, her desire to protect her brother at all costs, her determination to stand surety for him, her need of a solicitor to draw up an agreement.

When, at the end of an hour, Dr Shaffi gave her the name of a Mr Engles whom he thought might help her, she thanked him profusely. He felt, on leaving, she looked suddenly much more human, her face, with its dark beady eyes and hooked nose, less witch-like. He thought of what she had told him about all that had taken place at Castlebury Rings when she was younger. He wondered whether, on her next visit, he might . . . Then, as swiftly, he rejected the idea. He was well aware he was not a qualified practitioner and looked upon as something of a charlatan. But his practice was most lucrative. He was doing too well to take any further risks. He had to be discreet. Many of his patients were titled. Most wished to remain anonymous.

After he had said goodbye to Gertrude, he rearranged some papers on his desk and rang for his secretary. He knew he was now in for a far less interesting session. His next patient was Lady Avery, but he realised she was well worth cultivating. She had greatly increased his clientele.

9

SUMMER rain fell on the countryside around Netherford Halt as Dora stepped out of the train and the guard deposited her box on to the small wooden platform. Fred Penny wasted no time in getting his daughter and her belongings into the trap. Apart from a cursory greeting, to which she responded with equal brevity, they remained silent during the short journey, although it was a little more circuitous than usual. Dora was well aware that her father was taking a different route because they were less likely to pass so many people or so many homes, less of a target for prying eyes behind twitching curtains.

She looked neither to right nor left until they swung into Dr Forman's back entrance and she saw her mother standing at the front door of their cottage next to the stables. Then, as soon as Fred brought Punch to a halt, she burst into tears, jumped down and ran into her outstretched arms.

"There, there, child." Edith drew her into the only living room, where a kettle of boiling water was ready on the hob for the essential cup of tea. "Thee must be tired after thy journey," she went on, busying herself with producing the only positive aid she could think of at that moment, spooning plenty of sugar into the cup before placing it in front of her daughter who sat, after the initial weeping had subsided, scared and mute. Fred, having brought her box indoors and taken it upstairs, had now gone out again.

Presently, Edith broke the silence. "Thee in trouble, Dora?"

Barely audibly, the girl replied, "Yes, mother."

"What 'ave 'e been and done?" Edith was only now beginning to allow the possible awful truth to creep into her mind. "Is it . . . is it . . . ?" She faltered and her question remained in the air.

"Yes," was all Dora whispered.

The older woman gave a short gasp. Then, once again — although this time trembling all over — she came and

84

put her arms round her daughter.

"Who be the father?"

There was no answer, simply a fresh bout of weeping.

Edith frowned. "Someone you met on your half day?"

The weeping continued. There was still no answer. To give Edith Penny her due, she stopped catechizing. The girl was tired out. It would be best to wait until she had recovered a little. Perhaps even to wait until they had received a further letter from Miss Gertrude. Edith was thankful that all her other children had left home. There was no one else to pester her daughter and she knew that Fred would be unlikely to say anything, preferring to leave his wife to deal with the situation. It might be better to let Dora go to bed for the rest of the day, rather than for the three of them to face a silent wretched evening together.

Dora herself seemed only too thankful to disappear upstairs into the tiny room which she had been used to sharing with her now married sisters. She pulled a nightdress from her box, put it on and then, huddled beneath the bedclothes, lay shivering, even though the day was warm and, the rain having ceased, sunlight came slanting through the latticed window. She could hear the sounds she had been used to all her life — footsteps on the cobbled street, men and women calling to each other, Dr Forman saying something to her father in the stable yard, a soft whinny from Punch — and somehow their very familiarity eased her tension a little. At least the immediate ordeal was over. Her mother knew and had not rejected her. But would her father? Dora believed she had once heard him telling his wife that if ever any child of his brought disgrace on their home, they should never set foot in it again.

Dora did not hear him come in. Mercifully, she fell asleep and man and wife were careful to talk in whispers for the rest of the evening.

Fred, unable to eat any of the bread and cheese Edith put before him, eventually came out with, "What did she say, Edie?"

"'Tis a baby," was all she answered.

"Whose?" Although his voice was

lowered, it was savage, vindictive.

"She never said."

He was silent. Before he had even asked the question, he knew, without proof but without a shadow of doubt, who was the father of his coming grandchild. A hate welled up inside him such as he had never known. What could he say? What could he do? There would be no question of marriage. In any case, he wouldn't want Dora tied to a scoundrel like Claud Kimberley. He wasn't fit to be in the same room as her. He lifted his dark angry eyes and stared at his wife. "We must stand by her, Edie," he said, "but, my God, I'd like to kill the man who's done her wrong."

When Gertrude's second missive arrived by the afternoon post the following week, Edith, afraid to open the envelope alone, waited until the evening when Dora had gone to bed — the girl seemed only too anxious to lie down whenever she could — and Fred came home from work. Together, they pored over the various contents, bewildered by the long words used by Gertrude and even more bewildered and scared of the even longer ones in the solicitor's letter, together with an accompanying agreement which, it would seem, required some kind of assent. Had it not been for the intensely personal nature of the documents, they would have straightaway asked Dr Forman to help them, but shame kept them locked in private grief for three whole days and nights.

From what they were able to make out, it appeared that, because Dora was a minor and under the care of Miss Gertrude Kimberley, the latter was willing to pay two shillings per week during the pregnancy — should this be confirmed by a doctor — and three shillings per week thereafter should Dora be delivered of a child, this allowance to cease when the said child reached the age of fourteen or earlier in the event of the mother's marriage.

Troubled and puzzled as they were Fred and Edith realised that Gertrude was prepared to take some responsibility for what had happened. That, alone, confirmed what they had discussed over and over again since Dora's return. Claud Kimberley, himself still a minor, was the father of the child, even though in all the correspondence there was no mention of his name, nor, for that matter, any other allegations as to paternity. As gently as she could, Edith had tried to draw the truth out of Dora but, with astonishing stubbornness despite her distress, she refused to tell her mother anything else.

"She's scared, scared of Miss Gertrude, I reckon," Edith said to her husband, one evening when she had walked down to the Formans' vegetable garden where Fred was hoeing some early carrots. "It seems as how she never told her either." "An' that 'ud suit Miss G. fine, wouldn't it?" Fred answered gruffly, before straightening up.

Gertrude had, indeed, been very careful not to cross-question Dora once the ghastly truth had dawned on her. Certainly, she realised her staff would suspect but, so long as she got Dora out of the house before the girl made any statements or accusations, the better. What a mercy it was, Gertrude kept thinking, that Claud was about to go to Laverton Hall where, amongst other jollifications, he would be escorting some debutante daughter of Lilly Hennessey's cousin to a dance in the district. With his charm and good looks, he seemed to be in constant demand nowadays and, because of his uncle's continued patronage, it would appear that he had no difficulty in escaping from duty whenever it suited him, especially when, as in this particular instance, there was more than a little nepotism involved. The season was getting well under way and when Gertrude had remarked on his popularity, Claud had laughingly passed it off with a kind of mock modesty, saying, "Let's face it, Gertie, the mothers and chaperones like the fact that we've got a Buckingham Palace telephone number."

Sometimes she became concerned that he was so often asking her for an advance on the income he received from the trust set up under his father's will; also that he seemed to be burning the candle at both ends. But just at the moment she couldn't have been more grateful that his social life would be claiming him for well over a week. It should be quite easy to let him know, when he came home, that she had found it necessary to engage a new parlourmaid, owing to the fact that the one from the country had not been able to stand up to the rigours of town life.

Gertrude guessed that her brother would hardly be likely to enquire further. Nor did he. As always, she had smoothed the way for him. Dora Penny's somewhat precipitate departure was something which he would, she knew, be perfectly capable of pushing down into his subconscious. He would be only too glad 'not to know'.

And whatever allegations Dora might make as to the father of her child, Gertrude felt that by fully accepting responsibility for the girl's welfare, she had somehow cleverly pre-empted — so far as the Kimberleys were concerned — such a much worse situation.

10

CLAUD KIMBERLEY and Elizabeth Forbes-Jamieson made a pretty picture as they waltzed together at Meredith Place on a warm early June evening. Lilian Hennessey, sitting between the girl's mother and a certain duchess, watched them covertly. Her cousin's daughter could do a lot worse. True, the Kimberley boy was young but, thanks to her husband, he had good prospects. He had a wonderful opening at the Palace. With any luck, he would end up with a knighthood. He might be only a rector's son, but he had had a good education and seemed to know his way about. His manners were faultless. She suspected that Elizabeth was already more than a little in love with him. She was no beauty but she had nice eyes and not a bad figure. *The Blue Danube* came to an end and Lilly saw them disappear out on to the balcony. She trusted they would not go further. Elizabeth had her reputation to think of and Claud was Lilly's nephew by marriage.

At that moment Claud was, in fact, urging his partner to go quite a bit further than the balcony and she was more than happy to comply. Once outside the perimeter of the lights, he took her hand and led her down a path bordered on either side by a high yew hedge. Under the cedar tree at the end he stopped, took her in his arms and kissed her, thrilled to feel how readily she responded. His life seemed to be getting better and better these days. He was gaining confidence with the opposite sex all the time. Since taking Dora's virginity he had hoped it might be possible to tumble her into bed again whenever the opportunity arose. He had found her resistance, and the way he had brutally managed to overcome it, strangely exciting. It was a new experience which had nothing to do with kissing Elizabeth. That was quite a different thing altogether. He felt he now knew exactly what he wanted from different classes of women and just how to obtain it.

Presently, when Elizabeth suddenly

became aware that it might be circumspect to return to the mêlée, he led her back on to the dance floor and they performed a most accomplished foxtrot to the strains of *Tea for Two*. He was delighted to think that in the coming few days they would be seeing quite a lot of each other at Ascot — where they were meeting up with Gertrude — another ball and a large garden party at Laverton Hall, to which the Hennesseys appeared to have asked friends from far and wide.

When Claud came home to Lower Grosvenor Place, although looking somewhat jaded, he was full of all he had been doing. It was at least twenty-four hours before he noticed a rather older and sharp-featured parlourmaid waiting at dinner. "What's happened to Dora?" he asked his sister, nonchalantly, when they were alone having coffee in the drawing-room. "I sent her home," Gertrude replied, equally casually. "I'm afraid she was proving unsatisfactory. London didn't suit her." He nodded, holding out his cup for some more coffee. "I suppose the cockney ones are best, from the work point of view," he went on, mentally noting that he would have to look elsewhere for the kind of sexual satisfaction he required.

He had taken the change as Gertrude had known he would. She felt there was hardly likely to be any more trouble with the new domestic, so far as her brother was concerned.

Nevertheless, she remained worried about him, both because of his obvious weakness for the opposite sex, as well as alcohol. He was constantly pestering her to provide cocktails, something she had until now managed to resist. She supposed he was no different from a lot of young men, although she sensed he was less able to withstand temptation. There was, moreover, a third problem: the way he allowed himself to become so often overdrawn at the bank. She wondered if marriage to some sensible girl might help. Elizabeth Forbes-Jamieson seemed eminently suitable by all accounts. But they were both so ridiculously young. Besides, she herself did not fancy being relegated to the top floor flat quite so soon and watching some chit of a girl trying to manage staff. In many ways, she was glad to think that she had more or less undertaken to keep that part of the house available for visitors for at least three years.

Gertrude found that, apart from the unfortunate crisis over Dora, she was enjoying being in charge of a London home more and more. She felt she was learning a lot, becoming quite a woman of the world, in fact. Her social life was increasing daily and her weekly sessions with Dr Shaffi an added bonus. She felt that he found her attractive both mentally and physically, especially after she had revealed details of her youthful affair. Sometimes she thought about Reginald and wondered how his marriage was faring and whether he had ever told his wife about what had happened on Castlebury Rings. Most likely not. She knew he had children and could only suppose that he had settled down to become a sober and respected general practitioner like his father. Even Gertrude herself found it hard to connect the character she now was with the young woman who had succumbed with such abandon to Reginald's exciting method of seduction. When she had conducted her last painful interview with Dora Penny she had managed to ignore the fact that she was passing judgment on a member of her own sex for a fate which could have happened to her and for which she would have been much more to blame. She had gladly given in to Reginald's advances. In her heart of hearts she suspected, or rather, *knew* that Dora had not been seduced willingly by Claud.

Claud. Her thoughts invariably centred on him. She hoped the Pennys would be sensible about accepting the allowance she had offered. Mr Engles had stressed that, once this had been settled, any formal agreement would also include a clause to the effect that from then on there would be no further claims nor any contact between the parties involved. At last, Gertrude felt, she would be able to wipe the dust of Netherford off her feet. She would remain on Christmas card terms with the present incumbent for a while, but in due course she would let even that drop. Whatever had happened to the Penny girl would be a thing of the past.

On the whole, Gertrude couldn't help congratulating herself on having managed the whole unfortunate incident extremely well. Of course, it had been a stroke of luck that, thanks to Dr Shaffi, she had been put in touch with Mr Engles. He was obviously a clever little man, although his office was on the seedy side and Gertrude hoped that the rest of her dealings with him could be done by post and she would not have to go there again.

She was incapable of visualising the distress in the Penny household which her brother's actions had engendered. When her thoughts happened to stray in that direction, she quickly diverted them elsewhere. Naturally, she had no means of knowing that, at last, Fred Penny had taken his courage in both hands and gone to Dr Forman telling him, haltingly, the whole story while at the same time giving in his notice. Sidney Forman, shocked and devastated, refused to accept the latter. "You and Edie," he had said, solemnly, "cannot leave us, leave Netherford. You belong here."

"Not any more." Fred had replied,

curtly. "The missus wants to go and that's an end to it."

Edith did want to go. She knew people were already talking, all over Netherford. She knew what they were saying, even if she did not actually hear them. "Dora Penny's up the spout." "The Penny girl is in the club." It was more than she could bear. She had not spoken a word of reproach to her daughter. Nor had Fred. They both believed that what had happened to Dora was not her fault. They would stand by her, even though she refused to name the father of her coming child and however much Fred had previously laid down the law about any of his offspring who might bring disgrace on the family.

For her part, Dora had shown remarkable determination in stubbornly refusing all attempts to drag from her any mention of that terrible afternoon when Claud Kimberley, whom she had worshipped from afar, appeared to turn into another human being altogether. Occasionally, in her innocent, forgiving mind, she wondered whether he had been overcome by madness, had suffered some kind of fit, like the poor Shergold boy at Netherford who was sometimes unable to control himself and did funny things. In spite of all that had happened, she knew she would never betray Mr Claud nor, for that matter, Miss Gertrude. Her employer had been obliged to send her home and, according to her parents, was willing to make some provision for her and her child; although over this Dora had more than once heard raised voices arguing in the living room after she had gone to bed.

"We'll need the money," she heard her mother saying. "Dora won't be able to earn for a while." To which Fred had thundered. "I'll not sign, never in a million years." When Edith had murmured something about thinking of the bairn and how it would come in useful, Fred had banged his fist down on the table and thundered even louder. "We've raised six bairns, ain't we? What's one more?"

Part Two

11

ELIZABETH KIMBERLEY knelt on the floor in the drawing-room of Number 20, Lower Grosvenor Place, playing snakes and ladders with her seven-year-old daughter. It was getting on for six p.m. on an early autumn evening and she wished her husband would return from the Palace in time to see Daphne, before her nannie came to take her up to bed. But she doubted that would happen. More and more, Elizabeth was becoming resigned to Claud's increasing penchant for a life completely separate from that of the domestic family one she had tried so hard to create.

It had never been easy right from the beginning. Once the initial changes had been made after her marriage to Claud in 1922: Gertrude installing herself in the top flat, the servants all relegated to the basement so that their former quarters could be turned into a day and night nursery for the children she longed to have, and a large connubial bedroom, plus dressing-room and spare room created out of Claud's and Gertrude's erstwhile apartments, she began to find Number 20 something of a prison. It was a constant worry on her mind. Yet she knew it was not so much the house and staff, as the attitude of her husband coupled with the presence of Gertrude — even if she did not see her sister-in-law every day — which troubled her most. In some extraordinary way, even an unseen Gertrude had the power to make her feel as if some stern warder was constantly looking down from above, blaming her for Claud's increasingly late return home, Daphne's bilious attacks or the new cook/housekeeper's extravagance.

When Elizabeth and Claud had first announced their engagement, Gertrude had given them both her blessing, maintaining that she would be only too happy to retreat to the top flat and that she had no intention of interfering in their lives in any way, other than to help out if and when needed. After the wedding, however, the new young mistress of Number 20 discovered this to be far from the case. Although Gertrude kept to the bargain of only sharing Sunday lunch with them unless specifically asked on some other occasion, Elizabeth soon became aware that in some uncanny way nothing that happened in the house escaped the older woman. The pretty glowing bride turned into an apologetic anxious young wife, while feeling inwardly angry and distressed that her husband invariably seemed to take his sister's side if ever there was the slightest difference of opinion.

When Elizabeth became pregnant early on in the marriage, the situation deteriorated further. She suffered from prolonged sickness, which gave Gertrude the opportunity which it would appear she had been waiting for. Under the guise of only wanting to do her best to help, she discreetly took over the reins of Number 20 again, while Elizabeth retired to her bedroom feeling too wretched and exhausted to protest. When, at last, she began to feel better, the pattern seemed to have been set.

"You ought to be jolly grateful to the old girl," Claud said, one evening as they were preparing for bed. "After all, she does know the ropes. And she understands about children. She more or less brought me up after our mother died. You'll find her very useful when the baby arrives."

When the baby arrives. Elizabeth wanted a baby more than anything else in the world and could hardly wait for the birth. To a lesser extent, she was also looking forward to resuming marital relations with her husband again. But the doctor had warned her that she must take extra care throughout her pregnancy and rest was essential. Therefore during the daytime she spent many hours lying on a chaise longue in the bedroom, wondering what Gertrude was up to and when Claud would come home. With hindsight, she realised it was then that his habit of 'dropping in at the club' — as he put it — started. She was too artless and ignorant of the ways of men to appreciate that most of them were unable to forgo sexual satisfaction for any length of time.

It was not until some years later that she began to suspect that Claud did not always 'drop in at the club' on his way home. It was not until she had tried to get hold of him because Daphne had been rushed to hospital with acute appendicitis, that she knew for sure he had been lying about his whereabouts in the evenings. When the child was out of danger, she had asked him where he had been when she had telephoned Pratts. Only as she saw him hesitate and turn to look out of the window, mumbling about having had to visit an associate at the Palace, did she realise that he was trying to hide something.

She had never questioned him again. She had been brought up to believe that a wife should remain loyal to her husband whatever his own peccadilloes. She comforted herself with the thought that she had her heart's desire: a beautiful daughter. She had been warned by the doctors that she must never have another baby and therefore Daphne became infinitely precious to her. Neglected by Claud and overshadowed by his sister, she lavished all her care and loving attention on her only child.

It was almost more than she could bear

when, to her surprise, Claud suddenly came home earlier than usual on the evening she had been playing snakes and ladders with Daphne but, as soon as the little girl had been taken up to bed by her nannie, he had said, accusingly, "You really must stop mollycoddling the child. You ought to invite other children to play with Daphne instead of yourself. The Robertson kids are about the same age. It would be better if she played with them rather than her mother."

Something seemed to snap in Elizabeth's hitherto controlled acquiescent manner. "It might also be better," she retorted, acidly, "if Daphne's father spent a little more time with her."

Claud's expression darkened. He was not used to being put down by a woman. "I see as much of my daughter as any man in my position," he replied, pompously. "In fact, I was thinking of driving us all down to Brighton this Saturday in the new Hispano-Suiza."

Elizabeth was mollified. She had no means of knowing that Claud's early return and offer of a family outing was entirely due to the fact that his mistress happened to be out of town. She knew that Daphne would be ecstatic when she heard what her father intended doing. Her spirits rose. They would take a picnic. She would get Mrs Chambers, the new cook/housekeeper, to make one of her famous veal and ham pies. A picture of family life as it ought to be lived danced before her eyes. Only when Claud added, "No need for Nannie to come. We'll take Gertrude," did her fleeting glimpse of happiness fade as fast as it had arrived.

The day was hardly a success. Daphne had never been on such a long journey and was car sick before they reached Brighton. Unable to eat at the picnic, she became listless and fretful. In the afternoon, Elizabeth did her best to keep her amused in one of the shelters along the front, while Gertrude and Claud went off for a walk; but she was relieved when — albeit fearful of a repeat disaster — they started back to London.

After she had put Daphne to bed — the nannie having been given the day off — she came downstairs to find Claud and his sister deep in conversation in the drawing-room. They broke off when she entered the door and she knew they had been talking about her. Gertrude, with what Elizabeth could only think of as a forced attempt at tact, excused herself on the grounds that she had some letters to write. After she had gone upstairs, Elizabeth's temper got the better of her once again.

"I take it you were discussing your wife with your sister?" she remarked.

"Yes, but Gertie only wanted to help. She wondered whether you and I shouldn't go off for a holiday together. Decent of her, I thought. She would be perfectly prepared to hold the fort here. See that Nannie looked after Daphne properly. All that sort of thing."

"And what did you say?"

There was a fractional pause, which Elizabeth was quick to notice.

"I said that it was good of her and I would keep it in mind. The trouble is we're deuced busy at the Palace just now. Another state visit coming up. Maybe after Christmas. We might go down to Monte, say about mid-January."

"Perhaps you've forgotten," Elizabeth

answered, this time quite levelly, yet there was no mistaking the sarcasm in her voice, "January 15th will be Daphne's birthday. I wouldn't want to be away just then."

12

DORA BASSETT and her three children, Rose aged nine, Leslie aged five and little Pauline coming up three, sat round the table in a pleasant semi-detached house in the small town of Market Winton. In a chair by the fire, her father, Fred Penny, sat quietly drinking a cup of tea and watching the family, not without a certain satisfaction. His one regret was that his wife, Edith, was not alive to see how well things had turned out for their youngest daughter.

When Dora had been sent home from London by Miss Gertrude Kimberley ten years before and Edith, mortified by the reason, had insisted on her husband giving in his notice to Dr Forman, the Pennys had moved some thirty miles from Netherford to a remote Berkshire farmstead where, thanks to the doctor's kind auspices, Fred had obtained employment as a groom/gardener to an elderly widowed gentleman farmer. Fred knew that he was lucky to have got another job so easily at his age, but it so happened that his new employer was a good friend of Sidney Forman who told him the reason for the upheaval and that, although Fred was getting on, he was capable of doing more work in a day than the average young man would do in a week. Moreover, Sidney had jocularly used the old country expression, "He'll see you out!"

So the Pennys and their belongings were transported by carrier to their new home where Fred, though greatly missing his former employer, gave of his best to his new one. There was little gossip about Dora, for the cottage was fairly isolated and they kept themselves to themselves. The trouble was that Edith had never been able to come to terms with what she considered to be a family disgrace. Day by day, she saw her unmarried daughter becoming larger with child, a child for which she and her husband had proudly refused to accept any maintenance from Gertrude Kimberley, to the latter's annoyance and regret. But while Fred and his daughter also came to accept the situation, Edith silently grieved and fretted. She watched Dora so vigilantly that she even became aware when the baby started to kick. Her hitherto pleasant demeanour gave way to a deepening depression. More often than not, it was Dora who cooked the midday dinner, while her mother lay on her bed upstairs, staring straight into space as if she was not quite sure where she was.

Once the infant was born, she became even more strange. She would stand for a long time at a stretch gazing down at her small granddaughter, as she lay in the drawer of an old chest which had been turned into a makeshift cot. Eventually, her mother's behaviour began to get on Dora's nerves.

"Rose is all right, Mum," she kept repeating. "She's a healthy baby. There's no need to watch her."

But Edith would turn and stare blankly at her daughter, before walking away muttering something about the sins of the fathers.

When little Rose was two years old, Edith Penny was taken away to the local asylum. She had made an abortive attempt to strangle her granddaughter. Fred and Dora were devastated. Together they did their best to carry on, Fred working harder than ever, Dora keeping house and looking after him and her baby. It was then that she had got to know a young chemist in Market Winton, to which she occasionally went, pushing Rose in an old perambulator, in order to buy certain necessities such as gripe water for the baby or a mustard plaster for her father's lumbago.

Aware that she wore no wedding ring and conscious of her plight, one evening Edward Bassett offered to escort her home, as the shop was about to close and it was beginning to get dark. Dora accepted gratefully, for she did not relish pushing Rose the three miles over rough ground in the fading light.

Thereafter, Ted — as he asked her to call him — became more attentive, often turning up after hours with whatever he felt she might require. On such occasions Dora would produce a simple meal and Ted would spend the evening with her and her father. When, a few months later, Ted asked her to marry him she became nervous and confused. "But I have a child," she said. "That makes no difference," he replied. "I'd be happy to take on the little one and give her my name. She's a bonny lass. I'd be a good father to her."

For the first time since Claud Kimberley had raped her, Dora wondered whether to tell Ted Bassett the exact circumstances connected with Rose's birth. She decided to do so that same evening as they set out to walk up to the woods above the cottage, leaving her sleeping child in the care of her grandfather.

Hesitantly, Dora brought up the subject but, to her surprise, Ted cut her short. "You don't need to tell me anything, Dora," he said quietly. "I don't want to know. All I do know is that Rose is a good baby and her mother is a good woman, and a beautiful one." Gently, he began pulling her down on the short springy turf and started to kiss her. For the first time in her life, Dora became aware of what it was to know the love of a good man.

They were married that summer, though not before Edith and Fred

Penny's employer had both died. It therefore seemed perfectly natural for Fred to move into the house in Market Winton with the newly-weds where, anxious to keep his self-respect, he became a much sought after jobbing gardener. Ted Bassett prospered, so far as the times allowed, for the depression of the late nineteen twenties looked set to continue into the thirties. Rose, a clever girl, gained a scholarship to the local grammar school. She had the makings of a beauty, like her mother, though without the latter's sweetness of expression. There was something bold and flamboyant about her manner and, with puberty, she became very conscious of how people — especially boys — turned to look at her in the street. Tall and fair, she was the exact opposite of her half-brother and half-sister who were both short, dark-haired and shy. It was now that Rose began questioning Dora about her birth.

"Dad isn't my real father, is he?"

"No." Dora became wary.

"You had me before you were married, didn't you?"

"Yes."

The two of them were alone, the younger children in bed, Ted and his father-in-law at a political meeting. Dora was sitting by the fire, darning, thankful that she was able to bend her head so that Rose could not see the colour rushing to her cheeks.

"Who *is* my father?" Rose stared at her mother, accusingly.

"I'm sorry. I can't answer that question."

"Why? You must *know*, surely?"

"I decided it would be better never to talk about it."

"But that's not fair. I have a right to know, haven't I?

This time Dora looked her daughter straight in the face. "Not yet. When you're older. Meanwhile, you have the best stepfather anyone could wish for."

"Yes, that's as maybe. But he's not my flesh and blood."

"He is better than that."

"Meaning that my real father had *bad* blood, that *I've* got bad blood?" Rose came and stood over her mother now. Her eyes were bright, her expression disdainful. Dora suddenly realised what a

119

striking resemblance she bore to Claud.

"It means nothing of the sort," she replied, levelly. "Please get on with your homework."

With alarm, she watched her daughter flounce out of the room. Presently, she heard the front door slam. The memory of the afternoon when the child had been conceived came back to her, startling in its clarity. It might have been yesterday. She recalled her bewilderment, the pain, the way Claud had got up and left her with a curt warning to 'change the sheets'. She sat quite still, the darning in her lap. She was not a clever woman as she sensed her eldest daughter was going to be, but she was wise beyond her years. She prayed to God that Rose would never suffer the same fate which had overtaken her.

13

AS the nineteen thirties wore on, Gertrude could no longer ignore the fact that her sister-in-law was unhappy and that her own brother was the cause. But it did not occur to her that she, too, might have been a contributory factor to the unfortunate situation in Number 20, Lower Grosvenor Place. Gertrude, in middle age, reckoned that she was a steadying influence on the young couple, that she had, to some extent, curbed Claud's profligacy — albeit he had, for some time, been in total command of his own inheritance — and that without her presence Elizabeth might well go to pieces. She also felt that Daphne was profiting from the time at weekends which she gave up to improve the child's general knowledge, by taking her on visits to art galleries and museums or special places of interest in the capital.

Actually, Daphne was not particularly

keen on any of these activities. She preferred staying at home and writing strange little poems and stories in a notebook which she kept hidden at the back of a drawer in her bedroom. But she was a dutiful, rather nervous child and politely went off with Gertrude because she felt it was what was expected of her.

Claud had initially wanted his only daughter to go to boarding school, but had backed down, partly because Elizabeth, for once, put up such a strong resistance to the idea and partly because he suddenly realised that by sending Daphne away his wife would have more time on her hands — they had now dispensed with a nannie — and it would make it difficult for him to absent himself quite so often.

He had by now become increasingly involved with a woman called Valerie Cohen, who lived in a flat in Notting Hill for which he paid the rent. She was the daughter of an East End tailor and his wife, who had run away from home at fourteen, been raped (twice) by fifteen and gone on the stage as a chorus girl at sixteen, thanks to an impresario who had kept her for a further two years before turning his attention elsewhere. From then on she had lived by her wits and her undoubted sex appeal, using both to maximum advantage.

Claud had met her at a supper party after enjoying a music-hall to which he had been taken by a friend. Before the evening was out he had offered to escort her back to some rooms near Shepherd Market, where she was then living. As soon as he had climbed up the steep stairway and followed her into her front door, it seemed to him that she knew instinctively the kind of services he required. Within a very few minutes she had simulated the resistance which Dora Penny had once done with such pitiable earnestness. Only when Claud was close to frenzy did Valerie Cohen allow him to enter her.

From then on he was entirely at her mercy. He arranged her removal to Notting Hill and assuaged what little conscience he had by telling himself that she was necessary to his well-being. Without her he would be far less able to fulfil his husbandly and paternal duties. Elizabeth would find him more agreeable and remain entirely ignorant of his sado/masochistic inclinations. The occasional sex which they continued to have would reassure her that he still loved and respected her, even if the whole exercise had become, unbeknownst to him, something in which Elizabeth simply felt obliged to take part.

Moreover Valerie, Claud realised, appealed to his sense of danger. He had never been particularly brave or adventurous in the war and had regretted this. A medal would have added to his stature. Now, regularly performing an exciting clandestine game with his mistress made him feel more alive, more courageous, more of a man, in fact. He congratulated himself that even if Elizabeth ever did suspect some other liaison, she would have no knowledge of its deviant form or intensity, nor of the woman who provided it.

But in 1935 disaster struck, as it was more or less bound to have done, sooner or later. It was a Saturday and Gertrude had taken Daphne to an exhibition at the Royal Academy, oblivious of the fact that her niece could hardly have been expected to appreciate the paintings of the Impressionists at her age. When they got home Gertrude was not altogether surprised to be greeted by Mrs Chambers in the hall, for she knew that Elizabeth had gone down to the country to see her mother who was not well. She had imagined that Claud would have driven her, as he usually made some sort of effort to act the family man at weekends. When Mrs Chambers said that Mr Kimberley had been taken to St Mary's Hospital in Paddington, and that she had been unable to contact Mrs Kimberley because Sir Charles and Lady Forbes-Jamieson's telephone appeared to be out of order, Gertrude, ever capable in an emergency, asked her to take care of Daphne, threw herself into a taxi and reached St Mary's within a quarter of an hour. Enquiring after her brother, she was taken up to a small waiting-room on the third floor where she was confronted by a woman with a badly bruised eye and smoking a cigarette. Without having to be told, Gertrude knew at once she was Claud's mistress.

"You are waiting for Mr Kimberley," Gertrude said, flatly, more as a statement than a question.

"Yes."

"What has happened. How ill is he?"

Valerie Cohen had the grace to blush under her heavy white make-up. Her black hair, parted in the middle and pulled severely back from her slightly heavy face, reminded Gertrude of a woman about whom certain people close to the Throne were beginning to talk: Mrs Wallis Simpson. Had Gertrude had a little more insight or self-awareness, she might also have appreciated that Valerie Cohen was not altogether unlike herself, a fact which had not escaped the former. Although Claud had rarely mentioned Gertrude, she had always suspected that his admiration and dependence on his sister had sexual overtones which had been transferred to his mistress.

"He had a heart attack," Valerie answered bluntly.

"Is he, was he, conscious?"

"Not in the ambulance. I know nothing more."

A nurse entered the room and looked,

hesitantly, from one woman to the other.

Gertrude rose. "In the absence of Mr Kimberley's wife," she said, imperiously, "I am his sister, his next-of-kin."

The nurse nodded. She quickly realised that the woman with the black eye could hardly be a relation. Looking straight at Gertrude, she said, "Perhaps you would follow me."

Valerie Cohen made no attempt to rise or accompany them. Bold and self-confident as she may have been in different circumstances, she knew her place when it came to the Establishment. In fact, she had become rather tired of that stratum of society with its demanding arrogant ways. That was what had been the cause of today's horrific turn of events. Having recently met an older, richer and gentler paramour, a retired businessman who was prepared to set her up in a far more salubrious part of London, she had told Claud that she wished to end their relationship.

Hurt, incredulous and totally unused to not getting his own way, he had turned nasty, calling her all sorts of names which she had no idea he had ever known. To get her own back, she had taunted him by saying that he was still a child when it came to sex. He had then attacked her with such ferocity that she had feared for her life. Bruised and beaten, she had lain on the bed while he had ravaged her for the last time before passing out.

14

DORA BASSETT sat in Dr Evesham's surgery, trying to keep a fretful Leslie amused. His ears were blocked up with wax again, something which had afflicted him since infancy. She had left Rose in charge at home, warning her to switch on the gas oven and put the shepherd's pie in at seven o'clock and start getting Pauline ready for bed if she was not back by then.

Looking round the surgery, Dora doubted that she would be. The inclement weather of early March had resulted in more than the usual proportion of the inhabitants of Market Winton and its vicinity requiring the attention of their much revered doctor.

Dora thought back to her own youth, when Dr Forman had been her family's mentor and source of income, as well as doctor. He had been a good kind man, she recalled, and Dr Evesham was one of the best, too. Her husband, Ted, was constantly telling her that he considered there wasn't a finer practitioner in the south of England. He would make up the medicines which Dr Evesham prescribed, wrap the bottles in stiff white paper bound with sealing-wax — it was still the time before pills took precedence — and, one way or another, knew almost as much of the physical and mental troubles of the entire neighbourhood as the doctor himself.

When Leslie had, to her relief, miraculously become engrossed in a comic, Dora picked up a somewhat tattered newspaper dated four days earlier. It was not one which she would normally have ever read but, having nothing better to do, she found herself staring at the obituary columns which, in those days, were on the front page. *Kimberley*, she suddenly saw, *Claud, aged 36, much loved husband of Elizabeth, father of Daphne and brother of Gertrude. All enquiries to Messrs Allington, Lower Sloane Street, London SW1. Memorial service to be announced later.*

Slowly, she read the words again and the colour rushed to her cheeks. How extraordinary that she should have chanced on them like this. Rose's father was dead. Surreptitiously, she did something which, in ordinary circumstances, she would never have dreamt of doing. She tore out the relevant notice and was so concentrated on re-reading it once again that the receptionist had to call her name twice before, with confusion, she pushed it into her handbag, gathered up her other belongings and propelled Leslie ahead of her into Dr Evesham's consulting room.

Gently and expertly, he syringed the boy's ears, enquired after the rest of the family and gave Dora what she felt to be one of his kind, professional, once-over looks, before wishing her and her son goodnight. He had always taken a particularly fatherly interest in the Bassetts. He had known, of course, from the beginning that Rose was not the chemist's daughter, but he had respected man and wife's reticence on the subject. He thought tonight that she seemed uncharacteristically agitated and

131

wondered what had upset her.

Dora, for her part, could not get the news of Claud's death out of her mind. It was not that she felt any grief. In many ways, she realised that it might make things easier, if and when Rose asked more questions about her father. She would be able to inform the girl he was dead. Tonight, after she got home, as she watched her bending to pull the shepherd's pie out of the oven, noticed her rounded limbs, the too tight jersey straining over her swelling breasts and the way she casually tossed her fair hair back from her face after she had laid the pie on the table, Dora felt more than ever that she was harbouring a cuckoo in the nest.

Later on, after they were all in bed, Ted drew her to him and said, "What's the matter, Dora? Is it Rose?" He had been aware for some time that the girl was troubling her mother. Not for the world would he have added to his wife's anxieties by telling her that Rose was also troubling him, albeit in a rather different way. Only a few days ago, when he and his stepdaughter had happened to be alone in the house, she had suddenly and alarmingly asked him if he would explain to her the facts of life.

Taken completely by surprise, he had replied, "That is for your mother to do, Rose." "But Mum's too bashful," came the quick retort, "even if she has had three kids." He recalled getting up, unnerved, and starting to leave the room, saying, "Your mother is a wonderful woman, Rose, and a very good one." Before he had had time to close the door, he heard her second riposte, "That's the trouble. She's too good, although I suppose she must have fallen from grace once upon a time, having me."

Outside, to his dismay, he had found himself trembling. He had not wanted to admit it to himself, but the presence of Rose was beginning to disturb him profoundly. She was now fifteen and a very mature-looking fifteen at that. She was self-assured and immensely provocative when it came to the opposite sex. He had caught her more than once gazing at him with lowered eyelids and then, when she knew he was looking at her, she had turned away with a secretive smile. Did she *know* what she was doing to him, in spite of having requested information on the facts of life? Or was she — and here he had tried hard, but failed, to suppress the thought — hoping he might give her more than verbal instruction? Worse still, would he have enjoyed doing so?

He had begun to pray that somehow something would happen that would remove Rose from their midst. She wouldn't be going into service like her mother. That was out of the question. She was destined for higher things, was working for her school certificate which she would be taking in the summer, a year younger than most of her contemporaries, because she was advanced in mind as well as body. If she passed, and Ted had no doubt that she would do so with flying colours, then perhaps he could afford to send her away to college. He would certainly do all he could to that end.

Tonight, as he held Dora in his arms, he became frightened that perhaps his wife had sensed something of what was tormenting him and that was why she had seemed so distressed herself. Could she possibly have suspected that he was physically attracted to his stepdaughter? If so, he must put that right, at once, reassure Dora that all was well between them. Without waiting for an answer as to what had upset her and, naturally having no knowledge of her chance discovery of Claud's death, he began to make love to her in a way he had never done before. He took her forcefully, almost angrily, trying to obliterate the fact that this was how he would like to have taken Rose.

After Ted had fallen asleep, Dora lay awake for a long time. Her husband's unexpected precipitous love-making both puzzled and scared her. Why, he had not even waited for her to reply to his question. When she, too, slept, her dreams were wild and uneasy. Claud seemed to be raping her all over again, Gertrude appeared to come and go like a Cheshire cat and then Dr Evesham was telling her she was pregnant.

In the morning she woke, heavy and depressed and praying that her last dream would never come true. Mechanically, she got breakfast, saw Ted off to work and the children to school. It did not help when Rose called over her shoulder, "Shan't be in this evening, Mum. I'm going to the Craigs." Dora did not altogether approve of Rose's friendship with Bertha Craig, but she was sensible enough to know that any further attempt to discourage it would have the opposite effect.

Once the house was quiet and she and her father were on their own, she made some fresh tea and they sat drinking it in the small back room where she had put a match to the fire. She was grateful for his quiet undemanding presence, as if he, too, sensed she was disturbed but was too wise to probe.

She was suddenly overcome by a strong urge to tell him once and for all, the facts concerning Rose's conception. She knew that he *knew*, as her mother had known, yet a strange determination never to confirm their suspicions still held her back. Besides, she thought, what good would it do now? He was seventy-five. She had been aware for some time that he seemed thinner, shrunken. Once or twice she felt that Rose's wayward manner shocked and saddened him. She thanked

God that her mother had not lived to witness it. She wondered where she had gone wrong in the girl's upbringing, whether, if she had been firmer, she could have guided Rose along more satisfactory lines. Yet somehow she did not think she would have the same problems with Leslie and Pauline. They were far more biddable, so very much Ted's children whereas Rose was so very much Claud's.

Although Dora had never heard of the countless theories which pundits put forward concerning nature versus nurture, it seemed to her that heredity must be the strongest factor in the make-up of mankind.

15

GERTRUDE had imagined that, after she had been shown into the little waiting-room at St Mary's, she would soon be taken to Claud's bedside. However, after an interval which seemed like an hour but was, in fact, only ten minutes — during which time she and Valerie Cohen made no further attempt to prolong their initial brief conversation — she found herself being escorted along a passage where, at the end, she was ushered into the office of the Sister in Charge of the third floor. Starched, white-capped and omniscient, she rose, shook hands and motioned Gertrude to be seated. Only then did it begin to dawn on her that there might be worse to come. As soon as she heard the words, "I am sorry to have to tell you . . . " she realised, with horror, what must have happened.

"But so *young*," she kept repeating.

"Yes. But heart failure can strike at

any age. And there was a war wound it would seem," came the reply.

"But it should not have affected my brother's general health." Gertrude stared at the woman, hostile and deeply shocked.

"One can never tell." Sister Templeton regarded Gertrude out of piercing but not unkind eyes. She had briefly seen the woman who had accompanied Claud in the ambulance, who had looked as if she might have been beaten up but, wisely and tactfully, she made no reference to this.

"Mrs Kimberley?" she asked, gently.

"My sister-in-law has gone to the country to see her mother. It would appear the telephone there is out of order. I do not expect her back until later tonight."

"And then you will break the news?"

"Yes."

"Mr Kimberley will be laid out in our Chapel of Rest. If you and she would like to visit at any time, you have only to ask. Would there, by any chance, perhaps be a male relative who could take charge?"

Gertrude thought. She knew that

women were not really considered capable of dealing with death. Often they were actively discouraged from attending funerals. She herself might have been the mainstay of her father's demise yet it was, she recalled, her brother and her uncle who had appeared to carry the most weight, especially the latter.

Now, she supposed, Guy would have to be summoned again. He was getting on, but he was still perfectly *compos mentis*. She would get in touch with him as soon as she had spoken to Elizabeth.

She had been surprised at her sister-in-law's reaction. She had expected tears, helplessness and gratitude for all Gertrude was doing or prepared to do. But Elizabeth had accepted the news with calm and dignity. In the course of the next few days, she proved to be amazingly resolute, efficient and seemingly not in need of consolation. It was she who composed the obituary notices, told a subdued and wide-eyed Daphne that her father had died, held long conversations on the telephone with Guy Hennessey and instructed Mrs Chambers to prepare a

140

simple cold collation for the mourners after the funeral.

Deprived of her role as the family's guardian angel, Gertrude retired to her flat and sulked. Elizabeth, she thought, had no right to behave in such an authoritarian self-controlled manner. Gertrude felt that her erstwhile — and, as she had imagined, indispensable — assistance, was now being rejected in a most callous and ungrateful way. She feared for Number 20, for her flat, for her status as general adviser and such fears were exacerbated by the constant communications from the Palace, addressed directly to her sister-in-law.

It appeared that no pressure would be brought to bear so far as a date for Mrs and Miss Kimberley to vacate their home, although there was a vague verbal reference from the head of the King's secretariat, as to possibly nine months or a year. Mrs Kimberley, as the widow of a highly respected and valued Palace official — Gertrude couldn't help wondering whether the adjectives owed more to Guy Hennessey's patronage than Claud's actual usefulness to the Establishment — was told that she could have the choice of an allowance and a small apartment at Hampton Court or a lump sum should she wish to make a home elsewhere. Pending her removal from Number 20, every effort would be made to help her, both financially and practically.

Elizabeth did, in fact, wish to move back to the country, somewhere near her parents. She had never altogether taken to town life and she had no desire to bury herself amongst what she knew would be an elderly community at Hampton Court. What she wanted was a small house or cottage, within reasonable proximity of a good public day-school for Daphne. What she definitely did *not* want was any place large enough to accommodate Gertrude whom she feared, for all her seeming self-sufficiency, might still want to maintain some kind of close link with her.

Actually, had Elizabeth shown any signs of requiring her sister-in-law's support, Gertrude might well have considered the possibility of joining her ménage, but Elizabeth's sudden show of independence disconcerted her. It was as if Claud's wife was almost relieved at his death. Could she, Gertrude wondered, have known more about his mistress than she had ever appeared to do? Certainly, she had accepted Gertrude's diplomatic statement, that he had collapsed in the street, with extraordinary sang-froid. She had never enquired further as to why he had been in the Notting Hill area when picked up by the ambulance and Gertrude had, as always, been careful to save her brother's reputation by absolving him from any scandal, maintaining to the last, the image she had created and built up for him since he was a small boy. She did her best to dismiss from her mind the strange unsightly woman whom she had briefly met at St Mary's who had, mercifully, made herself scarce after Gertrude had been taken to see the Sister. She neither knew her name nor cared, so long as no stigma was ever attached to her brother's name.

Especially was Gertrude anxious that Daphne should be left with a memory of a father of exemplary character — the one thing, it would seem, about which she and

Elizabeth were in total agreement. During the months which followed Claud's death, Gertrude continually referred to him in Daphne's presence as "Your dear late father", or "Your devoted father", or "Your wonderful father who had always been prepared to give his life for King and Country".

Daphne, now thirteen, accepted these glowing commendations with a certain degree of surprise but also pride. She had known her father had been wounded in the war, but she had never considered his job 'round the corner', as she thought of it, as actually serving the King. She was unaware what his duties were, except that they kept him out of their home a good deal but also gave her and her mother and aunt the advantage of being allotted special seats at any kind of royal show or parade. Now, aided and abetted by Gertrude, she began to see her father in a different light. Far from mourning his death, he became an elevated figure in her mind, a kind of hero. She was pleased to find that her school friends regarded her with awe, especially when photographs of Claud's memorial service appeared in

The Illustrated London News, thanks to the determination of Gertrude to see they were published there.

Never having been particularly close to her father when he was alive, Daphne became far more interested in him now that he was dead. She would ask Gertrude to tell her more about their respective childhoods, about Netherford Rectory, about the grandfather she had never known and how and why her father and aunt had come to live in Lower Grosvenor Place. She did not ask her mother such questions, partly because she realised that Elizabeth would not have known all the answers and partly because she did not want to upset her in any way. She felt her mother was being extraordinarily brave.

Talking to Daphne about Claud's early years brought back many memories to Gertrude. Sometimes of an evening she would stand looking out over the rooftops of London recalling, with nostalgia, the place where she had grown up. She had been glad enough to leave it after her father's death and she certainly had no wish to return, but her niece's interest was gratifying. She wondered what the rectory looked like now, who was the incumbent and who the local doctor, for she had noted in *The Times'* obituary columns that both Dr and Mrs Forman had passed on. Then her thoughts switched to Reginald and their youthful capers on Castlebury Rings.

Inevitably, sooner or later, her mind turned to Dora Penny, unwelcome as that memory was. Over the years she had done her best to blot it out but now, the realisation that her brother must have fathered a child some fifteen or sixteen years ago began to trouble her profoundly. Somewhere there must be a boy or a girl a little older than Daphne. She prayed that the existence of a half-brother or a half-sister to her niece would never come to light. Thankfully, there had never been another word from the Pennys since their refusal to accept the generous — as she thought of it — allowance which she had offered at the time of Dora's 'fall'. There was hardly likely to be any communication now, thank goodness. Elizabeth and Daphne must — and surely would — remain in total ignorance of something which had happened so many years ago.

Gertrude was sorry that, Elizabeth having elected to live in a small house in the country, she would no longer have the pleasure of helping to steer her niece in the way she thought she should go. She would miss taking Daphne on educational visits round London, but she consoled herself with the thought that the child would probably come to stay with her during the school holidays. Unlike Claud, having managed her finances well, Gertrude was now negotiating for a small house close to Harley Street, where she would be able to keep up with her friends and acquaintances. It did not enter her head that there were far more of the latter than the former. Welbeck Mews would be a good address and she had always been attracted to the medical world. Although she had long given up seeing Dr Shaffi, she had now progressed to a Dr Zawila, whom she consulted every so often. He was a refugee from Poland and she couldn't help feeling that, rather like Dr Shaffi who had suddenly ceased practising in somewhat unexplained circumstances,

Dr Zawila admired her, in a perfectly platonic way, of course. She was past sex, she told herself, but she was still interested in it — if in what she failed to realise was a somewhat prurient fashion. She found the growing rumours about the Prince of Wales and Mrs Simpson quite fascinating.

16

THE parents of Elizabeth Kimberley, though grieved by the death of their son-in-law and their daughter's early widowhood, were nevertheless pleased to think she would soon be coming to live relatively close to them at Meredith Place. Both wholeheartedly supported Elizabeth's choice of home, Alverton Lodge. It was small but attractive and they felt she would make it more attractive still, owing to her new-found confidence and determination to lead her own life. Dulcie Forbes-Jamieson was also delighted that she would have the opportunity of seeing so much more of her one and only grandchild who was going to Parkside that autumn, a school some six miles from Alverton Lodge, which had an excellent reputation and took both boarders and day girls.

Charles Forbes-Jamieson had other more personal and private reasons for approving the move. He had never altogether trusted his son-in-law and had long suspected that he kept a mistress. It had not surprised him when, a little after the marriage, Elizabeth seemed to lose the radiance which had been so palpably evident when he had escorted her up the aisle of St Margaret's, Westminster. He had also had a strong aversion to Gertrude and was more than relieved to think she would now be remaining in London. He had always thought she was a far too forceful, even sinister, character and that it had been a mistake to have had her living virtually on top of the young couple. Although he had never believed in meddling in other people's affairs, he had once touched on the subject when he had been dining with Guy Hennessey at Pratt's. He had sensed that the latter was slightly embarrassed, as he tried to defend the situation, saying that he was sure his niece was most tactful and would be a help rather than a hindrance. Thereafter Charles, who was all for a quiet life, went back to the country and held his peace. He simply continued to concern himself with the running of his small estate, his shoot, his wife's neurasthenia and his own increasing arthritis.

Charles Forbes-Jamieson had great faith in his doctor, who lived some distance away in Market Winton. Dr Evesham, besides his usual panel patients, occasionally took on various private ones — even if they were not living strictly within the area of his practice — who were happy to pay well for his services. He would regularly drive over to Meredith Place, where he was regaled with tea and toast or tea and cucumber sandwiches, as befitted the time of year. During each visit he would take his patients' pulse and blood-pressure, prescribe medicines if necessary and possibly recommend the efficacy of taking the waters at certain spas in the south of England. He would also, on occasions, have a little talk with Lady Forbes-Jamieson alone, reassuring her about a host of minor anxieties such as palpitations and allergies. At the end of every visit arrangements were made for the next one, unless there was any emergency meanwhile. Dulcie would consult her and her husband's joint engagement diary and suggest a date in about three weeks to a month's time. Dr Evesham, after agreeing to the date and jotting it down in his own diary, would then take his leave, driving slowly and carefully down the tree-lined avenue — he never exceeded thirty miles an hour even on the main roads — feeling he had enjoyed a pleasant interlude — he could hardly call it work — in his usual daily round.

It was after one of these occasions, soon after Elizabeth Kimberley had moved to Alverton Lodge — something which he had been pleased to note had had a remarkably good effect on her mother's health — that he decided to call in on the Bassett family on his way home. The two younger children had been down with mumps and all the year he had been uneasy about Dora. She seemed to have lost weight and had been looking tired and strained. He was glad to find Pauline and Leslie much improved, their faces no longer like balloons. Dora also seemed better and her father, though quiet as ever, replied to Jack Evesham's enquiry after his health with, "Mustn't grumble, Doctor, not at my time of life." Both Rose and Ted appeared to be out. He guessed the latter was still working but that Rose was possibly engaged on activities of a lighter kind.

He was surprised when Dora volunteered the information that Rose was away. It was not often that she mentioned her eldest daughter, but tonight she seemed quite anxious to do so. "She got eight credits, Doctor, in her School Certificate," she announced proudly. "She's gone to live in Reading with Ted's sister, Mary. She lost her husband a little while back and she's finding life a bit hard one way and another. She'll be glad of the company, having no kids of her own. She used to be a school-teacher and she's back now teaching the little ones. Rose is helping her. Then, after Christmas, she's going to start taking a secretarial training at the new college in the town. Somehow, I think she and Mary will get on. Rose might have been . . . " here Dora hesitated before going on, "well, a bit of a handful sometimes, but she respects her aunt. Mary had a good education and Rose is all for learning. It could be the making of her."

Jack Evesham could not have been

more pleased or relieved. He had sensed for some time that Rose was at the bottom of the family's problems. Handled correctly he believed the girl had great potential. He had often wondered about her paternity. There was something about her which he could not quite define: a mixture of sensuality and superiority. It was if she was well aware that she did not belong in the Bassett household. He would dearly like to have known more, but he doubted he ever would. Of course, Fred could possibly have supplied the answer, but he was reticent like his daughter. Besides, Jack Evesham thought, as he made his departure, would it do any good for him to know? He was obliged to take life — and death — as he found it, to do what he could to help when he could. That was his role as a country doctor. There were times when he knew he was needed as a friend, confidant and adviser on matters not strictly medical; there were others when he knew it was wisest to refrain from probing and stick to purely physical symptoms. He was interested in all his patients, good and bad, rich and poor. Rather like a priest, he often thought of them as his flock. They made up the fabric of society. His practice was typical of countless similar ones in the England of that time.

Yet Jack Evesham was also very much aware of what was happening in the wider world far from Market Winton and its neighbourhood. He read the papers, he listened to the wireless. He didn't trust that man Hitler, ranting and raving in Germany. Ranting and raving were no solution to anything. It was the resort of hysterics. No one with any sense ever did that. And common sense was what Jack Evesham admired above all things.

He reckoned it was common sense which had prompted Ted Bassett to engineer Rose's removal from the household and take up residence with his sister, Mary. He had been sorry to learn that Ted's brother-in-law had died but, if he were brutally honest with himself, he felt it had been a blessing in disguise so far as the Bassetts were concerned. Rose would, of course, come home for holidays, but the pressure of having such an assertive and provocative young girl constantly in their home had been lifted. Ted Bassett had foreseen the danger and Jack Evesham could only admire his chemist's sagacity in taking steps to avoid it.

Dora, also, had much the same feelings towards her husband, together with gratitude. Ever since the night Ted had made love to her in such an uncharacteristically violent way, she knew what was wrong. Not for the world would either of them have admitted the truth. They were not a couple given to expressing their emotions in words. Until then they had been happy in each other's company and that of their two younger children. Dora had also marvelled that Ted had been such a good and forbearing stepfather to Rose and that, true to his promise before they were married, he had never asked her to tell him the identity of the child's real one.

But, as she had begun gathering Rose's things together ready to leave home, it occurred to her that perhaps now was the time to tell both Rose and Ted the true facts. She had been surprised that the girl had not asked further questions after her one attempt to discover more about her origins and, one evening as Dora was placing a framed photograph of the family at the bottom of her daughter's suitcase, something had suddenly prompted her to say, "Rose, I said I would tell you about your father when you were older. I think perhaps now that you are leaving home . . ."

She had been astounded by the quick, almost offhand response, which shocked her.

"Don't bother, Mum. I know."

"You *know*? But how?"

"Oh, Mum. You didn't think I wasn't going to find out, surely? I talked to Grandad."

"*Grandad*? But he never . . ." Dora's voice trailed away, as she sat back on her heels, incredulous and bewildered.

"No. He never *said*. Although I'm sure he *knew*. I just asked him to tell me more about when you were growing up at Netherford. He seemed quite keen to tell me. He must have loved working for that nice doctor. I thought it was strange that he and my grandmother suddenly upped and left the district and came here. Then I worked it out, put two and two together. When Aunt Edna came to see me, I got her to fill in about how you went to London with the rector's daughter." There was a pause. "And *son*," Rose added meaningfully. "Oh, don't worry, Mum. I haven't talked to anyone else about it, not even Dad. Sometimes I've thought he doesn't know, but even if he did he'd never let on. I'm not going to spread it around that I'm a clergyman's granddaughter, although I reckon you had a bad bargain. Even if his son didn't marry you, he could have done a lot more for you, wherever he is."

There was complete silence in the room, until Dora answered, quietly, "Your father is dead, Rose."

17

"I'VE asked Aunt Gertrude for Christmas," Elizabeth told her daughter one afternoon, as she drove her home from Parkside School in the new Morris Minor she had acquired since coming to live in the country.

"But I thought we were going to Granny and Grandpa's?" Daphne, rather like her mother, had become much more outspoken since her father's death.

"Yes, but they've kindly included her. We shall all go over to Meredith Place for the day." Elizabeth carefully refrained from any mention of the fact that her father would find it a strain. She had always been aware that her sister-in-law irritated him beyond measure. But what could she do? Gertrude was, after all, Claud's sister. She was alone in the West End of London and although Elizabeth knew there were many people with whom she kept in contact, she doubted they were close friends. Besides, Christmas was Christmas and Gertrude had yet to see Alverton Lodge.

Elizabeth was therefore determined to get the guest room just right for her sister-in-law's visit. She also wanted to give Daphne an early birthday party before she went back to school. The child seemed to have already made many more friends than she had ever done in London, and Elizabeth herself felt almost guilty about the much more convivial life she had begun to enjoy. She could not help noticing how well she seemed to get on now with all sections of the community, from architects and builders and domestic helps to local neighbours anxious to extend the hand of friendship — and she did not think it was just because she happened to be the daughter of Sir Charles and Lady Forbes-Jamieson.

When she had married Claud Elizabeth had been a shy virgin, expecting love and tenderness. What she had got was an immature petulant husband, used to getting his own way and who, although she had not known of the existence of sexual deviation, somehow made her feel she had failed him as a lover and that he wanted something she was unable to give. It was therefore hardly surprising that, starved of affection, she now responded eagerly to overtures from other people, many of which, she had to admit, came from the opposite sex and showed admiration for her, but in the most chivalrous and courteous way.

When she occasionally heard vague rumours from Palace sources about the continuing association between the Prince of Wales and Mrs Simpson, it made Elizabeth think long and hard about men and women's relationships. Somehow she could not connect Wallis Simpson with love. Her severe saturnine features reminded Elizabeth uncannily of Gertrude, although other than that, there was no resemblance. Wallis was slim, svelte, sophisticated and fashionable. Gertrude's figure, over the years, had become thick and set. She had taken to wearing somewhat mannish suits and little hats perched at a jaunty angle on her black — surely now dyed, Elizabeth thought — hair, which did not enhance her appearance at all.

Even though her sister-in-law had been born and bred in the country, somehow Elizabeth did not feel she would quite fit in with the kind of life she herself was now leading at Alverton Lodge. She was glad when Gertrude, while accepting her invitation to come for Christmas with a kind of cautious politeness, stated that it would be necessary for her to leave the day after Boxing Day, as she had several engagements in London from the 28th onwards. Actually, Gertrude had no such engagements, but she wanted to give the impression that she was conferring a favour by coming to Alverton Lodge and was in no need of any familial patronage on the part of Elizabeth.

Gertrude was, in fact, extremely lonely, although she would never have admitted it, even to herself. Having got her new home as she wanted it, with the help of a rather austere cook/housekeeper and daily housemaid, she managed to fill her time with a certain amount of good works. She maintained her association with Queen Mary's Needlework Guild, was on a committee for helping the poor in the East End and another for raising money towards a new hostel for fallen women in Lambeth. (Considering her experience vis-à-vis Dora, the irony of this escaped her.) She went to various political meetings, especially those in support of the League of Nations. She also became a member of the local library — she disapproved of the Left Book Club — where she nevertheless regularly took out books by all the best-selling authors of the day: Priestley, Maugham, Cronin, Wells and Huxley and, although she did not disclose the fact, began avidly to read crime novels, especially those by Dorothy Sayers. Quite often she would telephone some female she had known when living in Lower Grosvenor Place and suggest they went to a film or lunched at Fortnum and Mason. But it seemed to Gertrude that they were not quite so keen to know her as they had been when she was so closely associated with the Palace. They would make excuses and promise to ring back the following week, but the following week went by and no one got in contact.

Dr Zawila, sensing her depression,

suggested she might take a holiday or go on a cruise but, for all her self-assertiveness and seeming independence, Gertrude did not fancy travelling alone. She did not trust foreigners and was, in fact, xenophobic. (This was the only trait she had in common with Sir Charles Forbes-Jamieson.) It appalled her to think of having to worry over tickets and passports and foreign languages and what might be happening to her home in Welbeck Mews in her absence. She explained to Dr Zawila that she was going to spend Christmas with her late brother's wife and that she really had far too many engagements in London to take a holiday at the moment.

Dr Zawila was not fooled. After she had left him on this particular visit, he was sorry that she had felt obliged to lie to him about her social life. He wished he could do more for her other than, hopefully, give an hour's sympathetic hearing to relieve the symptoms from which many of his middle-aged, comfortably-off, unattached female patients suffered. He was no stranger to loneliness, his wife having left him several years ago, something he kept to himself. It would never do for a man in his profession to admit to personal failure in relationships. Besides, his 'ladies', as he thought of them, might start getting ideas. He realised that Gertrude was extremely obsessive and a controlled hysteric. Given half the chance, she might become a nuisance.

After Gertrude had left him that day, she regretted having lied to both him and Elizabeth about her fictitious engagements. If she hadn't, she might have been able to persuade her sister-in-law to let Daphne come back to London with her. They could have gone to a pantomime — *Peter Pan* perhaps — and resumed their educational jaunts. It had distressed her that she had had only two letters from her niece since they had last seen each other and that neither mother nor daughter appeared to be missing the benefits she had hitherto bestowed on them.

When they greeted her on Christmas Eve at Reading station, Gertrude was further put out because they both looked so extraordinarily well and cheerful. The sore throat which she herself had been trying to stave off with the aid of Friar's Balsam had become worse during her journey. She felt obliged to apologise for her hoarseness, which put her at a distinct disadvantage.

Elizabeth, hoping that Gertrude would not pass on whatever she was suffering from to anyone else over Christmas, did her best. As soon as they got back to Alverton Lodge she was glad to find that her one and only domestic help, a young girl called Muriel, had faithfully carried out all her instructions: tea was ready, logs burning brightly in the sitting-room grate and the gas fire had been lit in Gertrude's bedroom.

At six o'clock, on Elizabeth's insistence, Gertrude retired, almost meekly, to bed and was positively grateful for the hot toddy her sister-in-law brought her up soon afterwards. Having received Gertrude's assurance that she would require no further sustenance that evening and would now sleep off her indisposition, Elizabeth went back downstairs and telephoned her mother. Dulcie, while often giving the appearance of frailty and nervousness in everyday life, rose to the occasion when need be far better than most.

"Whatever happens," she said, "you must let Daphne come for Christmas. We've got the Patterson twins coming with their grandparents. You remember, their mother and father are in India. We'll send Bates over in the Daimler in the morning with a hamper of food and some of Cook's special broth. Then he can bring Daphne back. Pack a suitcase so she can stay the night. Yes, I quite see why you'll have to stop with Gertrude. I'm terribly sorry, my dear. Have you rung your doctor?" (Dulcie had always wanted Elizabeth and Daphne to become private patients of Dr Evesham, if he was prepared to make visits even further away. She had intimated that she would be only too happy to subsidise the arrangement, but here she had come up against her daughter's fierce and, she had to admit, admirable determination to be independent.)

"No. I thought I'd wait till the morning. See how she is," Elizabeth answered.

"Better to do it now, darling. You may find he's off duty. I think all the doctors in the district work a kind of emergency service over the holidays."

Elizabeth found her mother's prophecy only too true. On telephoning her GP she was told to ring another number, where a pleasant voice assured her that her husband would call at Alverton Lodge before eleven the next morning.

Elizabeth, having seen Daphne off with Bates and insisted that her maid-of-all-works must go home as planned, suddenly heard another car draw up outside the front door. On going to open it, she found a dark thick-set middle-aged man with nice eyes standing on the step.

"Mrs Kimberley? I'm deputizing for your own doctor for twenty-four hours. I live over the border, as it were, in Bucks. My wife tells me you have a visitor down with this wretched 'flu which seems to be going about."

"Yes. I think that's what it must be. How very kind of you to call."

"Not at all." He came inside, took off his hat and coat and she showed him up

168

to Gertrude's bedroom, standing aside a little diffidently as he went towards the bed. She knew that convention made it necessary for another woman to remain on hand while any examination took place. But what she was not prepared for was the unconventional greeting with which this strange doctor started proceedings.

"Good God," she heard him say, looking down on the figure in the bed, clad in a white long-sleeved flannelette nightgown, her dark hair spread out loosely round her flushed perspiring face. Elizabeth wondered whether Gertrude had taken a sudden turn for the worse.

Then, for the first time since she had arrived at Alverton Lodge, she saw her guest give a wry smile. "Why, Reginald," came the almost non-existent whisper, "I'm sorry you've caught me looking like this."

Part Three

18

IN early 1940, five months after the outbreak of the Second World War, Private Rose Bassett sat on her hard bunk bed in an army hut at Aldermaston, rubbing her stockinged feet. For the past four years she had become used to wearing high, or moderately high, heels. Now, she had been obliged to get used to flat-heeled lace-ups again, as issued by the Auxiliary Territorial Service. The cramp resulting from unused muscles was devastating.

In her twentieth year Rose had grown into a tall striking young woman, now immaculately attired in khaki uniform, which she had carefully altered so that it fitted perfectly. She therefore stood out amongst her contemporaries and was invariably chosen to be 'Marker' at any kind of parade. She considered it somewhat of a joke — albeit rather demeaning — to be drilled by a male sergeant major and found it hard to keep a straight face when he yelled, "Pick up yer feet, ladies. Pick 'em up. Left right, Left right, Halt! *Abaaat* turn."

After her initial training, Rose had elected to go into the clerical side of the Service. Her secretarial qualifications stood her in good stead, but she had no intention of remaining in the ranks for long. She was fiercely ambitious and determined to get a commission. She had confidence in herself, as well as ability, and had already held down a good job with an insurance company in Oxford, sharing a flat with three other girls. She had also, unlike most of her female acquaintances — who were either too scared or intent on waiting for marriage — lost her virginity. But she had been astute enough not to suffer the same fate as her mother. Unbeknownst to Dora, she had saved up enough money to visit a female gynaecologist in London, having been given the name by an older more sophisticated girl at the secretarial college, the daughter of well-to-do parents.

Since Rose had left home, she had had several boyfriends, but the relationships had never lasted long. She was not at all sure that she wanted to get married and she was *quite* sure she did not want any children. Had the word been in everyday use in those days, she would probably have classed herself as a feminist and been proud of it. In many ways, she was the female equivalent of her father from the point of view of how she treated the opposite sex. She was offhand and arrogant and, once she had made a conquest — especially when it was all too easy — she lost interest. Though not given to self-analysis, she was vaguely aware that part of her, deep down, wanted to vindicate the appalling suffering her father had inflicted on her mother.

On the other hand, she did not go home a great deal. She found Dora's sheer goodness somehow irritating. After Rose had found out about her paternity she had wanted to shake her mother for having accepted her 'lot', as she thought of it, so meekly. If Claud had still been alive, Rose knew she would have got in touch with him and made his life as difficult as possible, exposing him for the brutal shallow creature he must have been.

One day, when she had been pondering over this, it occurred to her that even if she could not challenge her father, she could well embarrass his family. She had gathered from the obituary notice which Dora had told her about that he had a wife and daughter, but she had no idea where they were now. When she had gone to London to see the lady gynaecologist, she had looked up the telephone directory and had found the name of Kimberley, with a 'G' after it, listed in the area she had been visiting. Annoyed with herself for not having gleaned more information from her mother, she had made her way to Welbeck Mews and seen a dark-haired middle-aged woman emerge from Number 3. But this, she realised, could not possibly be Claud's widow. Nor, because she looked so old, did Rose feel she could be the sister who had also been mentioned in the newspaper.

Thereafter, for some time, she had let the matter drop from her mind, but intermittently it had kept surfacing. The knowledge that she had a half-sister, whom she had never met, kept niggling at her. What was she like? Were *they* alike? How old was she? Had she joined the Services? What sort of a lifestyle was she used to? Was she rich? And, more importantly, did she *know* about Rose?

It irked her that this unknown female might be oblivious of the fact that she had a sibling of maybe almost the same age, albeit conceived on the wrong side of the blanket. It wasn't *fair*. Rose imagined her as a selfish, spoilt, uncaring individual, quite unaware that Daphne Kimberley was, at the moment, doing her obligatory initial fifty hours' training in a general hospital, preparatory to becoming a VAD in an emergency one near Aldershot; and that her mother had joined the Women's Voluntary Service, spending six days a week in a local centre, helping those in need to deal with the countless problems that war had brought into their lives.

Elizabeth Kimberley was, in fact, invaluable in her self-appointed task. Her charm, sympathetic attitude and common sense soon commanded respect from all quarters. If you wanted help, so word went about, you should get hold of Mrs Kimberley. When, at the time of Dunkirk, an SOS went out for volunteers to provide tea and sandwiches for the exhausted BEF arriving in overcrowded trains day and night on Reading station, en route to destinations which the authorities had yet to organise, it was Elizabeth who was at the forefront of the operation, often snatching a few hours' sleep on a hard bench in the waiting-room. "That woman," an old retired general from the First World War, remarked, "is a bloody miracle."

During the glorious summer of 1940, while England waited in suspense for Hitler and his armies to invade its shores, three other women whose lives had been affected by the late Claud Kimberley, also found themselves adapting to unprecedented circumstances. Dora Bassett, devoutly thankful that her son, Leslie, was still too young to fight, continued to care for two small evacuees from the East End of London, as well as working four mornings a week in the local NAAFI canteen. Her father had died early in 1939 and she now gave as much time as she could to the war effort while Ted, on top of working

177

long hours in the shop — without the assistance of two young employees who had been called up — became an Air Raid Warden every other night. Dora felt that she and her husband were closer than they had ever been. Since she had talked to Rose about Claud, it naturally followed that she had spoken to both Ted and her father and the relief at no longer keeping everything to herself had surprised her.

Sometimes Dora wondered just why she had been so silent on the subject all those years ago. Considering that her parents obviously knew, it would have been much better to have been open about it. She could only think that, in her naïveté, she had felt that by sparing them the distressing details, she could pretend to herself that they had never taken place, shut them out of her mind, forget that such people as Claud and Gertrude Kimberley had ever existed. Now, after all this time, she was able to look back on them dispassionately. Occasionally, she wondered what Gertrude was doing. She supposed that the woman must be in her fifties and a confirmed spinster, for it seemed unlikely to Dora that she had ever married.

Gertrude was, indeed, fifty-three and had taken a billetee of a slightly older kind than Dora's two little East-enders. She had given over her best spare room to a Major at the War Office, whose temporary headquarters were only a few minutes' walk away in Cavendish Square. Although she had now dispensed with the services of a resident cook/housekeeper, she felt that she was old enough for there not to be any misunderstanding about the situation.

Major Palmer was a thin, slightly severe-looking man whom she rarely saw, for he required no meals and left the house early in the morning and did not return until late at night, Sundays included. She gathered he had a wife up in Scotland, though no children; but she was unable to find out much about him because they seemed to live like ships that pass in the night. Moreover, she had her own special job which kept her fully occupied and suited her administrative skills. Thanks to Dr Zawila and her past record as a VAD in the First World War, she was now supervising the nurses' home near the Middlesex Hospital.

Not all that far away from Gertrude, Valerie Cohen, having sadly slipped more and more downhill, had retreated to a bed-sittingroom again in her old haunt of Shepherd Market where, although she had no shortage of uniformed customers, she feared her age was fast beginning to catch up with her. Sometimes, as she said goodbye to some stray individual for whom she had rendered the only kind of service she knew how to supply, a nameless terror overcame her. Then she would take a grip on herself, tidy her room, make a cup of tea, light a cigarette and hope that she could save up enough money during the war, or the 'duration' as some people called it, so that she might be able to get out of London and live a reasonable existence in the country after it was all over. She never doubted but that England would win.

Little or much, most of Claud's women accepted their diverse roles. Possibly his widow fared best. For Elizabeth was young, healthy, had no son to fear for and thrived on capabilities she had not known she possessed. Her daughter, though glad to have decided to nurse, felt constantly tired. Tall, tenderhearted and conscientious, she worried over her patients to such an extent that after the Battle of Britain the Matron at the emergency hospital was obliged to send her home on sick leave.

No such qualms of conscience, however, affected Rose, who was now stationed at Headquarters, Southern Command. Her troubles arose because of her growing anger with the authorities for their slowness in giving her any promotion. She was working in a pool of typists, the monotony of which was sometimes relieved by being called to the Operations Room to take dictation from a staff officer. The fact that she was singled out rather more often than most caused resentment amongst her associates and started her thinking that she might put her undoubted sex appeal to greater use than ever before.

She knew that a certain Colonel was friendly with her Company Commander, for she had seen them dining together in the local country club. Such socialising between male and female officers was commonplace. On the other hand, Rose was well aware that Colonel Fanshawe would rather risk his life than risk his commission by being seen out with another rank, let alone a private in the ATS typing pool. Nevertheless, she thought, if she went about it carefully, she might well obtain the promotion she was seeking by getting Bertie, as she knew he was called, to put in a good word for her in the right quarters. She became excited. It was a game she knew how to play. For the time being it completely took the place of any ideas about getting even with her half-sister.

In the autumn of 1940, as the blitz in London was at its height, Colonel Bertram Fanshawe became Rose's target number one.

19

DULCIE FORBES-JAMIESON, having been widowed soon after the outbreak of war, now seemed to have come into her own, rather as her daughter had done some years previously. It was not that Dulcie hadn't been devoted to her husband, nor he to her. She still missed Charles tremendously. But she had always been, despite her neurasthenia, the more resourceful of the two, a fact which few people recognised.

Realising that Meredith Place was far too large for her to continue living there alone, it seemed almost like a stroke of luck when she was approached by the Air Ministry who wanted to take it over as an RAF headquarters, having already commandeered some five hundred acres of flat farming land nearby, as an emergency airfield. Dulcie was only too pleased to retreat gracefully to what had once been the nursery quarters, together with her cook who had been with her for almost half a century. The two elderly ladies found the proximity of so many young men gave them much interest and provided a stimulus to their otherwise quiet and reclusive lives.

Elizabeth was not quite sure when the idea of fun and games in the erstwhile dining-room of her old home began to take shape, nor was she exactly sure who initiated it, only that her mother suddenly telephoned to ask when Daphne would next be home on leave as she would like them both to come over. "There is a nice Wing Commander," she said, "who is greatly in favour of providing as much entertainment as possible for his boys, so I suggested a tea-dance. They are installing a radiogram."

Elizabeth, intrigued and full of admiration for her mother's spirit, besides being anxious that Daphne should enjoy herself more, was delighted. She was worried that her daughter seemed to take life so seriously, that she found it hard to sleep while on night duty and was too tired to get out and about as much as her contemporaries. She knew that there was certainly no shortage of young men around, especially in the Aldershot district, and Elizabeth suspected that most of her daughter's friends were having, in spite of the war — or, rather, because of it — a very good time.

Down at Southern Command, Rose was at last enjoying herself also. With an expertise worthy of a top military strategist, things were progressing according to plan — her plan. Certainly, fate had played into her hands. Thanks to her smart appearance, strong personality and obvious competence, she had gained her first stripe and been put in charge of several other girls in the typing pool. One evening, when she had been working late, she happened to know that Colonel Fanshawe was still in the Operations Room — alone. With the excuse of going there to put some typing on another officer's desk ready for the morning, she thought at first that he had not noticed her. But as she was about to leave, he said, suddenly, "Lance Corporal Bassett," and she realised that he must all along have been conscious of her presence. It was an encouraging sign. She turned. Whereas another girl might have said, "Yes, sir?" Rose merely smiled, said "Yes?" and waited.

"I was wondering," he went on and then floundered, for until then he had not exactly been sure what he was wondering, only that he was weary, Rose was exceptionally easy on the eye and he wanted to retain her company.

"Is it more typing?" she enquired, with the same half innocent, half provocative expression on her face which she well knew had ensnared others in the past.

"Certainly not tonight," he replied, with an attempt at jocularity. "I think it's time we both knocked off. Do you often work as late as this?"

"Once a week," she replied, promptly, "although I've been told there might be a rush on soon."

"Oh, so you've been warned?" He felt on firmer ground now, although he was naturally unable to reveal that there was to be a mock evacuation of the Command in a few weeks' time to an empty country house in Wales.

"I wouldn't mind extra work," Rose volunteered, gaining assurance with every minute. "In fact, I'd be glad of it, especially if it's *different*."

"You find the typing pool boring?" he asked.

She stared at him this time with a whatever-do-you-take-me-for expression. Then she answered, with great deliberation, "I've never been so bored in all my life."

"I'm sorry." Bertie Fanshawe stood up. It was, he realised, necessary to end the conversation and she took the hint. But as she walked back down the stone steps leading to the dungeon — as the typing pool was called — Rose smiled to herself. She knew that some kind of rapport had been established. Sooner or later they would have a closer relationship.

To her regret, Gertrude envisaged no closer relationship between her and her elusive lodger. Major Palmer continued to come and go as unobtrusively as ever. It was not that she wanted more than an occasional friendly tête-à-tête. It was just that she would have welcomed a chance to offer him a whisky now and then from her stock of rationed alcohol. But Matthew Palmer remained something of a mystery, simply leaving polite little notes such as: 'I shall be going to Scotland this weekend', or 'I shall be away on duty next Tuesday night.' She therefore concentrated on devoting most of her energies to the nurses' home, astounded that so many young women — especially those on night duty — seemed completely shameless, shoving pillows down their beds in an attempt to deceive her into thinking they were innocently asleep during daylight hours.

Being now much more fully occupied, Gertrude had somewhat altered her previous way of life. There was, after all, a war on, as she said to herself. Having dispensed with any resident domestic help, she also thought it seemed a trifle indulgent to spend time and money talking to Dr Zawila, especially as there now seemed little to be gained from it. He had probably helped her most by recognising her undoubted skills and directing her into such worthwhile war work. Besides, she was slightly perturbed because he had become so involved in the pioneer work of a Jewish refugee at Staines, a so-called doctor who was putting servicemen to sleep for three weeks in his nursing-home as a cure for stress. Gertrude, although always interested in unorthodox medicine, did not altogether hold with such treatment. People, she considered, should be able to solve their problems through intelligent discussion rather than barbiturates.

Often, she recalled the extraordinary way she had met up with Reginald again when she had been staying with Elizabeth after she had moved to the country. It had been such a strange coincidence. She had been dismayed that he had caught her, literally, with her hair down and in her nightdress; but afterwards she couldn't help thinking about the times when he had seen her in far greater *déshabillé*. She had still never met his wife, but they had kept in touch and she had been grateful for his occasional letter, even one in which he had made an enquiry about the Penny family, asking if she knew what had happened to them. His friendship made her feel less alone, less forgotten, for although her sister-in-law was conscientious about telephoning and constantly renewing invitations to stay, she feared that she had less and less in common with both Elizabeth and Daphne and far more with this old friend of her youth.

She had answered Reginald's query about the Pennys as best as she could, simply saying that she had no idea what had happened to them after they had left Netherford. She told him that she had employed the youngest daughter for a time when she and Claud had gone to London, but the girl had proved unsatisfactory and she had been obliged to send her home. Reginald, naturally unaware that Dora was now a panel patient of another GP practising in a neighbouring county, merely pushed the information to the back of his mind and then forgot all about it. Even if he had known Dora's married name, it would have meant nothing to him. His enquiry had been a casual one to help fill up a page of writing paper. He had never been a particularly good or fluent correspondent. He preferred face to face confrontation or, possibly a little more than that, he thought wryly, remembering Gertrude and himself on

Castlebury Rings.

When Dora Bassett sat in Jack Evesham's surgery in early 1942 she, too, had forgotten everything for the moment except that she felt ill. She had no specific symptoms except sleeplessness and depression, although not for the world would she have told anyone they had come on after she had discovered a letter in the pocket of one of Rose's old coats, which made it quite plain that her eldest daughter was no virgin. Although she had always realised that Rose was flighty, she had never imagined that she was actually promiscuous.

Dora had felt shocked, hurt and bewildered, typically blaming herself for not having brought the girl up properly. She was also fearful. She had no knowledge of the careful steps Rose had taken to avoid pregnancy and she was desperate that the child should not suffer the same fate as herself. But, once seated in front of Dr Evesham, all she could say was that she was having difficulty in sleeping and wondered if she might be having an early change of life.

After a thorough examination, in which

191

he could find nothing physically wrong, except weight loss, he wrote out a prescription, but asked her to come back in a fortnight. He had no doubt that something was on her mind and guessed it had to do with Rose. After she had gone out into the cold March evening, he sat for a full two minutes before ringing for his next patient. Dora and Ted Bassett were more than just patients to Jack Evesham. He hoped that the younger daughter would be able to take care of her mother. It seemed to him that Dora needed a lot of support for the time being. If she did not pick up he supposed that Rose might put in for what was called a compassionate posting, so that she would be nearer at hand. But somehow he doubted it. He feared that Rose was more likely to take care of Number One.

20

ROSE BASSETT was, at that moment, dancing with Colonel Fanshawe at the Savoy Hotel to the tune of *Deep in the Heart of Texas*, played by Carroll Gibbons and his band. Rose was on a forty-eight hour pass and Bertie Fanshawe was on his way north for a week's leave with his wife. Rose was wearing a short black shiny dress she had bought that afternoon. They had a table by the dance floor, to which they returned every so often and looked at each other, anticipating the night ahead. It did not worry Rose in the least that Bertie was a married man. It made their assignment seem all the more exciting.

A hundred miles away, Elizabeth Kimberley was trying to persuade her daughter that she would enjoy the tea-dance at her grandmother's home the next day. "But I won't *know* anyone," Daphne kept saying. She was being quietly obstructive.

"But you will, by the end. It'll be fun. There's sure to be more men than girls, which is always a good thing. I believe some Americans are coming."

Daphne remained unconvinced. She was, her mother thought, stubborn but really rather beautiful, in a solemn restrained way. She reminded Elizabeth of some girl in an old-fashioned painting, a Botticelli, perhaps. Her light brown hair, parted in the middle and rolled up beneath her nurses' cap when on duty, now hung loosely round her pale oval face. Her brown eyes were large and grave. Except for her height, Elizabeth could see nothing of Claud in her daughter at all. She felt the girl took after her own mother with, just at the moment, rather less charm.

"What are you going to wear?" Daphne asked, suddenly.

"Oh, my old blue, I think." Elizabeth hadn't really thought much about herself. "But I wondered if you'd like a new dress," she went on. "I've got plenty of clothing coupons saved up. You're welcome to them. We might go into Reading tomorrow morning and have a look round."

194

Daphne brightened. Perhaps it would not be such a bad weekend after all. And she could certainly do with a new dress. In spite of never feeling exactly well, she had put on weight round her middle. The starchy food and the regular lifting by young nurses unused to the job, sometimes enlarged their waistlines. "Do you think Jason and Co. would have any silk stockings?"

"I doubt it, but we could try."

"One of the nurses at the hospital has been given some nylons by an American."

"Really?" Elizabeth wondered who the girl was and hoped the nylons had been honestly acquired. She had no doubt that her own daughter would get to the altar still a virgin, but she was well aware of the impact the American forces were having on British girls now that they had come into the war after Pearl Harbor.

When the two of them arrived at Meredith Place the next afternoon, Elizabeth was surprised to find the tea-dance seemed already in full swing. Wing Commander Robson greeted them warmly, taking her straight over to where her mother was sitting, while Daphne, looking rather fetching in the new dress they had bought that morning, was whisked away by a Pilot Officer on to the dance floor where a Paul Jones was taking place. Dulcie, dressed in grey chiffon, appeared to be thoroughly enjoying the proceedings, not at all put out that her granddaughter had not yet said "Hello". "They're so short of girls," she remarked. "You'll be the next one to be commandeered."

Sure enough, after the Paul Jones was over, David Robson asked Elizabeth to dance with him. It seemed like a pleasant but entirely new experience. It had been so long since she had taken the floor with anyone. She could hardly remember the last time it had happened. Even when she had been married to Claud, they were more likely to go out to dinner or the theatre or rather boring official receptions. In fact, she realised, her dancing days had been mostly when she was a debutante and had been thrilled to feel Claud's arms around her as they waltzed to *The Blue Danube*. Now, she prayed that she would not be expected to jitterbug and was greatly relieved when a slow foxtrot started to be played on the radiogram.

On the way home, Daphne said, "You made quite a hit with the Wingco," to which Elizabeth replied, "I didn't see you exactly behaving like a wallflower."

"No. I must say it was better than I thought it would be. That Pilot Officer who started me off has asked if he can come over to Aldershot sometime and take me out."

Elizabeth was delighted. She did not mention that Wing Commander Robson had made a similar kind of suggestion to her. She had been surprised, flattered but evasive. He had made no mention of a wife, although somehow she did not think he would have proposed meeting again if he had had one.

David Robson telephoned her a few days later asking if she would care to dine with him at a nearby roadhouse. She had not expected the invitation to come quite so soon, but she accepted because she liked him and felt that if it *did* turn out he was married, she could simply make an excuse not to go out with him again.

She knew that she could have found out from her mother, who would have been sure to know, but she did not want to ask Dulcie. It was so obvious that she was longing for Elizabeth to remarry.

On the appointed evening she dressed with care. He arrived exactly on time in a battered old car, for which he apologised. She was nervous at first, but as the evening progressed she found herself relaxing. Soon, questions and answers came easily. He seemed to know she was a widow — her mother would have seen to that, she thought — and presently he told her that he had lost his own wife during the Battle of Britain. "It was so . . . well, *unjust*," he said. "I mean, there was I simply trying to get the better of Jerry but she, poor thing, was worried sick and pregnant. Our baby wasn't due for another two months, but it was born prematurely. A little boy . . . who died. They couldn't get Frances to hospital in time."

He broke off and, instinctively, she put out a hand. Then he said, "Thank you," and for a while they were silent.

"I don't think I could ever marry

again," he went on, eventually, "not while there was a war on. It wouldn't be fair. I never realised that it's the ones who have to *wait* who are the hardest done by. When one is up in the air fighting the enemy, doing one's job, the adrenalin flowing, it's so much more easy. It's the ones left on the ground, often lying awake, waiting for the correct number of planes to return, counting, knowing when some of them are missing, they're the ones who suffer. Frances used to put up at a hotel near our base so as to be near me. It would have been so much better if she hadn't."

When he drove her back to Alverton Lodge she thanked him sincerely, but she did not ask him in. She felt sure that they would see each other again, but as friends only. She was grateful to him for making the situation so clear and would not have had it otherwise.

The next time she went over to Meredith Place her mother asked, with an attempt at casualness, whether she had seen any more of David Robson and she replied, equally casually, "Yes, I went out to dinner with him." "How nice, my dear," Dulcie said. "He's thought the world of here, you know."

Elizabeth was not usually short with her mother, but something made her say, swiftly, "I'm sure," and then quickly change the subject.

21

MATTHEW PALMER had left a note for Gertrude to say that he would be away on Monday, Tuesday and Wednesday of the following week, as he had to serve on a War Office Selection Board. It was unusual, she felt, for him to be quite so specific about his movements. She had no idea what or whom he would be helping to select and was agreeably surprised when, suddenly coming across him on the Sunday evening, he explained that he was required to assist in judging the eligibility of young women in the ATS who wanted to become officers. Gertrude, who had hitherto wondered whether her lodger might be in the Secret Service because of his reserved manner, could only suppose that he was probably in a more mundane branch of the Army, the educational side, perhaps. This was, in fact, correct. Academically brilliant, he was a thoughtful, farsighted individual, desperately concerned about what would happen to the youth of the country — that is, however much of it survived — after hostilities were over.

Gertrude, seizing the opportunity, asked him if he would care for a drink. Matthew Palmer hesitated. He was a serious man and had only ever looked upon his billet as a quiet convenient place where he would never be obliged to be sociable. He took his duties extremely conscientiously and was often tired at the end of each day. Nevertheless, he was invariably polite and Gertrude, standing in the hall in her neat navy blue costume, seemed to pose no threat.

"It's most kind of you," he replied, and she led him into her drawing-room. Here, feeling suddenly grateful for the unaccustomed after-dinner whisky, he expanded a little. "The girls who come before the War Office Selection Board, or WOSBIE as they call it," he said, "have already been considered by their COs to be officer material. My job is interviewing each one and assessing her potential with regard to aptitude and past records."

Gertrude, delighted to have at last buttonholed her elusive guest, listened attentively. It was the kind of stimulating verbal intercourse she craved. "What sort of questions will you be asking them?" she enquired, having poured herself a weak whisky and soda also and feeling very much a woman of the world.

"It varies," he answered. "Naturally a girl's background, scholastic achievements, previous occupation all come into it. Of course, one will have read their notes and the results of their written intelligence tests before one actually sees them. My task is only a fraction of the whole process. They have to go before a psychologist and take part in fairly extensive physical trials. It's all a bit gruelling."

"Do they come from all over England?"

"No. There are other centres, but the ones I shall be seeing come from units in the Southern Command. Those who pass go on to Officer Training Centres. I always feel sorry for the ones who are rejected. About a third of them are, unfortunately. The tough ones seem the most likely to get through, however academically brilliant the others may be. We're looking for leadership, someone other girls can have confidence in."

Gertrude was fascinated. After they said goodnight, she went to bed feeling more cheerful than she had for some time. She hoped that there would be more opportunities for other pleasant tête-à-têtes now that they had broken the ice. Matthew Palmer was not the taciturn stranger she had thought him to be. He was simply a shy, thoughtful, cultured man — and probably lonely. She would find out more about him, in time. She missed having a man to talk to more than she cared to admit. Dr Zawila and his predecessors had helped, but it wasn't like someone actually sharing the same roof. Claud, however unsatisfactory he might have been had given her a *raison d'être*, even after Elizabeth had come on the scene. Of course, if she had married Reginald, Gertrude realised her life would have been very different. Yes, very different indeed, she thought, as she struggled into her long-sleeved flannelette nightgown.

As for Matthew Palmer, he too was

thinking at that moment how different his life would have been if he had remained a schoolmaster, if he hadn't been a Territorial, if the war hadn't interrupted everything. He could well have been on the way to having his own prep school by now. Cynthia would have made a perfect headmaster's wife. It was a tragedy they hadn't been able to have any children. Young people had always interested him. That was why he had gone in for teaching. Youth was so full of life and hope, even now, while there was a war on. As he drifted off to sleep, he felt pleased to think that tomorrow he would be doing, at least in a roundabout way, the kind of work for which he had been trained.

He did not interview Rose until the second day of the WOSBIE. She came into his room, unobtrusively, rather as she had once come into the Operations Room when Colonel Fanshawe had been alone. Yet Matthew Palmer was instantly aware of her presence. There was something about her which commanded attention, especially the attention of men. Devoted and loyal as he was to his wife, Matthew felt oddly disturbed, as if it was this new aspirant who was sizing *him* up, rather than the other way round.

"Please sit down, Corporal Bassett." She had gained a second stripe by now.

"Thank you, sir." Rose sat. Was there, Matthew wondered, just the faintest hesitation between the 'thank you' and the 'sir'?

Playing for time, he shuffled the notes in front of him. Then he looked up again. "I understand you did extremely well in your School Certificate."

"Yes, sir." He was glad to note he could no longer detect any hesitation about the use of 'sir'.

"And then you went to secretarial college where again you did well."

"Yes, sir."

"And after that you held down a good job in an insurance company before you joined the ATS."

"Yes, sir. For over two years."

"Tell me, what made you join up?"

She seemed to have the answer all ready, as she replied, "I wanted to do my bit for the war effort." Naturally, she did not add anything about wanting to

206

see more of the world.

"Did you think of becoming an officer at the beginning?"

There was a perceptible hesitation before she replied, "I think so. I thought I had the qualifications and I might be of more use in an administrative capacity."

It was as good an answer as any, Matthew Palmer thought. Perhaps a little too pat. All the same, the girl was bright, full of initiative and confidence and incredibly smart. He could imagine less forceful characters responding to her, wanting to emulate her. She would be good in an emergency. He played what he often felt was his trump card. "Corporal Bassett, if some of the girls in your charge were on an Ack Ack site which was bombed, what would you do?"

"I'd telephone my commanding officer and go there as quickly as I could, taking as many helpers as possible, get them out, get them to hospital or a First Aid post, later notifying next of kin."

You couldn't fault this one, Matthew Palmer thought. She had it all worked out. He studied her carefully. He realised she must have been the candidate he had watched from the window the previous day, organising a mock stretcher party, pointing and telling the others how to lift a dummy body over a wall. He was sure she would make a good officer, although he did not think he himself would exactly like to have been under her command. There was not much compassion there, he felt. On the other hand, compassion wasn't really what the authorities were looking for. Before he brought the interview to an end, he said, "Tell me about your home, your parents."

For the very first time, his interviewee seemed slightly, but only slightly, ill at ease.

Then she replied, quietly, "My father is a chemist. My mother has not been well, but my younger sister is at home and able to look after her."

Thank God, Rose thought, as she walked down the corridor after Major Palmer's not too intensive grilling, Pauline could cope with Dora who, by all accounts seemed to be having an early and distressing change of life. Pauline was so different from her. She was nice and kind and gentle and willing. Her mother had had a raw deal in life but Pauline would be a great comfort to her and maybe she herself could help in other ways: she would go home on leave more often, write letters, send presents. She was no Samaritan but she would do her best. She wondered what Major Palmer would have said if she had told him that she was a bastard, whose grandfather had been a man of the cloth and whose father had been an important official in the King's secretariat at Buckingham Palace.

She had little doubt that she would pass the WOSBIE. It was a challenge which she enjoyed. None of the tests had seemed all that difficult and the interviewers had been perfectly reasonable, that is, except for the lady psychologist. Rose hadn't much cared for her. Still, she had given Dr Sprague as good as she got, and after the interview was over she had a feeling that somehow the woman had been impressed.

Travelling back to Southern Command, Rose was looking forward to telling Bertie Fanshawe all about it, although she knew that finding the time and place to see each other was becoming increasingly difficult. But she did not really mind if their relationship cooled down now. It had served its purpose. She knew that Bertie had put in a good word for her in the right quarters. There were plenty more fish in the sea. It would be easy to hook any amount of them, once she was wearing a Sam Browne.

22

"I'M sorry," Dora said, "that I wasn't able to get to your Passing Out parade."

"That's all right, Mum." Rose, home on leave before her first posting as a Second Lieutenant, was doing her best. She had been shocked to find her mother somehow shrunken, as if she had suddenly become old beyond her years. Guiltily, Rose realised that she was actually rather glad, considering what her mother was looking like, that Dora had not come to Windsor along with all the other relations and well-wishers. It had been embarrassing enough having Pauline, wearing Rose's old coat which she had failed to alter properly, so that her younger sister had stood out, a shapeless pathetic figure and distinctly ill at ease.

"Where are they sending you?" Dora asked.

"Portsmouth," came the prompt reply.

"*Portsmouth*?" That was a town which

had been badly bombed some time back, Dora thought anxiously. The Luftwaffe hadn't visited it so much lately, but one never knew. Dora, unlike Rose, had no knowledge of 'compassionate postings', but she thought it would have been nice to have had her elder daughter nearer at hand.

"Don't worry, Mum." Rose lay back on the sofa with her hands clasped behind her head. "Jerry's got to reckon with Second Lieutenant Bassett now. He doesn't know what he's up against."

In spite of herself, her mother had to smile. Rose's confident assurance in her own worth was, at least temporarily, a tonic. However much heartache the girl had caused her, it was impossible for Dora not to continue loving her firstborn. That part of her which had wanted to reproach, rebuke, warn and urge Rose to mend her ways, had been subjugated, at the cost of a nervous breakdown, which Jack Evesham — with the memory of Dora's own mother in mind — had told Ted could be serious and prolonged.

Dora had been obliged to give up working in the NAAFI. She no longer appeared to have the physical strength, let alone the mental resolve; and she was also thankful that her two little billetees had been taken back to London by their parents, now that the RAF seemed to be gaining mastery over the enemy. She therefore spent much time on her bed, leaving Pauline, who had left school, to look after her and the house.

Ted, prompted by Dr Evesham, did his best to find out what was going on in his wife's mind, but here he had come up against the stubbornness she had earlier shown towards her parents in her refusal to say just how she had become pregnant. He was sure Rose was at the bottom of things once again, but whenever he mentioned the girl, Dora became tight-lipped.

Long before she had found out about her eldest daughter's lifestyle — the letter she had discovered from someone called Ralph had been explicit and shocked her profoundly — Ted had suspected that Rose was no virgin. He regretted the way the girl had developed but he also felt that she knew her way about. Moreover, he had to admit to himself that she seemed astonishingly fit and happy. If Dora *was* concerned about her morals it was too late and he felt his wife was now worrying unnecessarily. Rose had come of age, she was off their hands. He was far more concerned about Pauline who had had to forgo, at least temporarily, any idea of training to be a hairdresser, and also Leslie who would soon be called up. He was surprised that the latter event did not now appear to take precedence in Dora's mind. She seemed to have got things out of proportion.

His thoughts turned to his mother-in-law. He supposed that obsession possibly ran in the family. He knew they were putting a lot on Pauline, but he was uneasy these days about Dora being left alone. If only she would *talk*. He could only hope and pray for things to improve. Often, he came home from work to find her carelessly attired, staring straight into space and it frightened him. Whatever happened, his wife must not end up in the same way and the same institution as her mother.

Apart from having unfortunately felt sexually attracted to Rose some years ago, Ted had always been a model husband, supportive and loyal, the best any woman could hope for. But now he was at his wits' end. Sometimes his job as air raid warden seemed like a welcome respite. As he walked the streets of Market Winton, occasionally having to yell "Turn that light out" when, perhaps, some usually conscientious householder had slipped up, it would take his mind off the situation at home. He had learnt to do with very little sleep now, sad that when he crept into bed towards dawn, his wife was still under the influence of the bromide which Dr Evesham had prescribed. He did his best to contain his frustration, but it would have been good to have been able to take Dora in his arms and resume the loving relationship they had hitherto known.

There was another man, not all that many miles away, who also felt it would have been good to take the woman he desperately wanted in his arms. Wing Commander David Robson had fallen deeply in love with Elizabeth Kimberley and he was fairly sure the feeling was reciprocated. Yet they were conducting an almost Victorian courtship, each determined to keep their relationship on a platonic footing.

He knew he was going to be posted soon and the fact made him both angry yet relieved. They couldn't go on as they were. Every time he went over to Alverton Lodge or took Elizabeth out he had wanted to make love to her. But she was not the sort of woman with whom he would have dreamed of having that kind of relationship outside marriage. She seemed to have all the qualities his late wife had possessed: a beauty of spirit besides physical beauty. But he could not, must not, ask her to marry him. Had he not told her soon after they met that for an airman on active service, marriage was not fair on any wife. It would not be fair now, *especially* now, however much he wanted her. He was going to Bomber Command. Cologne had just been flattened. The Ruhr was next on the list, he believed, and he would be in on that.

He called to see her in early July to say goodbye. It was a hot sultry evening and he found her wearing shorts and a sun top, weeding her herbaceous border. In spite of all her dedicated war work, she had always seemed to find time to care for the domestic side of her life.

As she heard his car turn in at the gate, she straightened up and came towards him. "Why, David, what a nice surprise." She had not been expecting him and, until a few hours ago, he had not been expecting to visit her either. His 'posting' had come through only that afternoon.

"Do come in," she said. "You're in luck. I've just been given some black market produce from Meredith Place! I'll make you some scrambled eggs."

He smiled and followed her into the house, while saying, "I haven't really come for a meal."

"Oh, but I insist. I'll just run upstairs and make myself a bit more presentable. Help yourself to a drink."

In her bedroom she stripped and went over to her wardrobe to pull out a summer dress. Only when she turned did she see him standing in the doorway. Slowly, he moved towards her. "I came," he said, huskily, "to say goodbye. I leave for Norfolk early tomorrow morning."

She was in his arms then. Afterwards, she thought it had not seemed wrong for either of them. All the pent-up emotions of the last months were swept aside in a passion she had not known she possessed.

23

DAPHNE KIMBERLEY stood in a call-box just outside the emergency hospital, explaining to her mother that Pilot Officer Ripley had asked her to go with him to a friend's twenty-first birthday party in London.

"But darling, I don't think . . . "

Daphne cut her short. "Please, Mummy. There hasn't been an air raid for ages and I could stay with Aunt Gertrude, couldn't I?"

"Well . . . "

"She's always said she'd put me up at any time," Daphne interrupted again. "Oh, I know she's got some chap living with her, no I don't mean *really* living . . . " Daphne went off into peals of laughter. "But I could sleep on the sofa, if necessary. It would only be for one night. Then Bill has to go on up to Yorkshire to spend the rest of his leave with his parents. I've found I can get off here. *Please!*"

Elizabeth was torn. It was good to feel how much more alive Daphne was these days. She knew the reason, naturally. Pilot Officer Ripley had done wonders for the girl. She had come out of her shell. But *London*. Of course, Gertrude would be the perfect answer. All highly respectable and above board. She would probably even stipulate the hour by which her niece must return but . . .

"*Please*," came the voice on the other end of the telephone again. "I'm running out of pennies."

"Well, I'll write to her," Elizabeth answered, though still doubtfully.

The line went dead. Elizabeth put down the 'phone. It would have to be done by writing, she thought. It simply wouldn't be polite to ask for this favour by suddenly ringing up. Her relationship with Gertrude was not as good as it might have been. On the other hand, Elizabeth realised, this would be an excellent opportunity to try to rectify matters. She had accepted the fact that Gertrude really did not seem to want to come to Alverton Lodge, although she did not think it had anything to do with the extraordinary coincidence before the war, when the stand-in doctor she had had to summon to her sister-in-law's bedside turned out to be an old boyfriend. The idea of Gertrude ever having had a boyfriend had caused both Elizabeth and her daughter endless speculation. Daphne had been quite fascinated. No, Elizabeth thought, it was just that she and Gertie were, and always had been, miles apart in every way. She wondered what on earth her sister-in-law would think now — and her daughter for that matter — if both knew that the seemingly respectable widow, dedicated to war work, concealed a far more libidinous woman underneath. Even Dulcie had absolutely no knowledge that David Robson and she sometimes managed to meet — and such assignations were far from platonic. When Dulcie had asked if she ever heard from "that nice Wing Commander", Elizabeth had merely replied, "Oh, just occasionally," amazed at her ability to deceive.

Now, here was Daphne, her own daughter, in love — or thinking she was — simply wanting to go to a party with the young man of the moment and willing, afterwards, to return to her aunt's house for the night. The liaison, Elizabeth felt sure, was extremely innocent. It seemed churlish to deny Daphne a little pleasure. She was working so hard and deserved it. The war was bad enough for people of her age, even though it had afforded them a great deal more freedom than had ever taken place in her own day. Yes, she would write to Gertrude, but even as she started the letter, she could not help thinking about the extraordinary transformation which had taken place in both her and her daughter's lives following that first tea-dance at her old home.

She was pleasantly surprised by Gertrude's prompt reply. 'As I believe you know,' she wrote, 'I no longer keep a resident servant and therefore have another spare bedroom.' The letter went on, however, to list various conditions, as Elizabeth thought it might: 'I take it that the young man in question will call for Daphne, as I should like to make his acquaintance. He has evidently met with your approval so I am sure he must be of good family.' Elizabeth could not help giving a wry smile at this remark. It seemed as if Gertrude was living in another era, especially as the letter ended with: 'I must ask Pilot Officer Ripley to bring my niece back by midnight, as I shall naturally wait up to see she is safely home.'

Still, if Daphne was so keen to go, Elizabeth felt sure she would abide by Gertrude's dictates. There was simply no other way she was going to allow her daughter to spend a night in London.

When Daphne heard the outcome of the correspondence she was ecstatic. Once again on the telephone to her mother, she said, "How super. Good old Gertie."

"You must take her a present."

"Yes, of course. I'll use my sweet ration. I'm on a diet, in fact."

After they rang off, Elizabeth sat thinking for a long time. She recalled what David had said about members of the Services — air force ones in particular — not marrying in wartime. She felt confused. She did not want Daphne to marry this young man. She did not want her to become so involved that the two of them felt marriage was the only solution; yet she wanted her to have as good a time as possible. Had there not been a war on, she supposed Daphne would have become a debutante, as she had been. She would have brought her out, as Dulcie had brought her out. Now, Daphne was being brought out in other ways. She supposed Bill Ripley was of good family, as Gertrude had intimated in her old-fashioned way. But she knew very little about him, other than that David had said he was a nice young man.

She was aware of being guilty of having double standards: clinging to the morality of the past for her daughter, enjoying the immorality of the present for herself. On the evening when Daphne would be in London David had said that he just might be able to spend it with her. She knew that he was going out over Germany regularly at night now but, thankfully, she never knew exactly when. She was glad she was not nearer to his base. She did not want to count the planes returning, as poor Frances had done.

Elizabeth realised that she had never felt this way about Claud. Certainly, she had thought she was in love with him in the beginning rather, she suspected, as her daughter felt she was in love with Bill Ripley. But Elizabeth could not recall feeling any actual sexual desire on her part. That was where, she supposed, she had failed her husband. Over the years she had gleaned rather more knowledge about sex. Sometimes she had speculated about the woman who had given Claud what he wanted. She had known much more about her than Gertrude had ever given her credit for, but she had kept quiet about it. Divorce seemed unthinkable in those days. Besides, there was Daphne to consider. Daphne had always come first, although since David Robson had come into her life she did not feel quite so sure about it. However anxious she might be about her daughter's forthcoming visit to London, she knew that if David happened to be with her that evening his presence would take priority.

In the event, he rang to tell her that it might be difficult for him to get as far as Alverton Lodge that night. Could she, perhaps, meet him on the previous one? He named a hotel in London.

"London?" she queried, although not fearfully this time.

"Yes, darling. Look, I haven't got a lot of time. Say you'll come."

"Of course," she replied and then repeated the name of the hotel. "I'll be there."

And if the Women's Voluntary Service want me for twenty-four hours, they'll just have to whistle, she said to herself, as she put down the receiver.

She had already left for London that day, when the matron of the emergency hospital where Daphne worked tried to telephone her to ask if she would come and fetch her daughter, as she thought a few days at home might help. Pilot Officer Ripley had not returned from a bombing mission over Germany the previous night.

24

ROSE was on a ferry going over from Portsmouth to Hayling Island. She had a suitcase full of cash to pay the girls in her platoon who were stationed there. She felt important but, unusually for her, slightly apprehensive, both about the amount of money she was carrying and taking charge of her first pay parade, with all its strict formality. Being an officer had quite a few unexpected responsibilities, as she was fast finding out.

There were, however, definite compensations, especially when off duty. Portsmouth seemed to be teeming with Service personnel of all descriptions. She had lost no time in getting to know a most handsome naval commander with whom she was having an affair, made all the more exciting because of an army brigadier who was also courting her favours. She much enjoyed playing them off against each other: Brigadier Archie

Henford knowing all about Commander Phillip Ross, although the latter knew nothing yet about the Brigadier. Rose realised that she was not popular amongst her female colleagues, but this had never bothered her. She knew it was the price one had to pay for being a man's woman.

She managed to write home fairly regularly, because she was well aware that the situation there was by no means a happy one. But she also managed to quell any pangs of conscience about not spending more leave at Market Winton by telling herself that there was nothing really she could do, that Pauline was coping wonderfully and that she was the daughter whom Dora loved and needed most.

This was not strictly true. Dora loved all her children, but in different ways. Pauline and Leslie had never given her any trouble and therefore the love she felt for them was of a simpler, secure, more passive kind. Rose had caused her fear and anxiety from the moment she was conceived and therefore the love Dora felt for her was fiercely protective.

She would excuse Rose's waywardness to herself, while privately grieving over it. This grief reached its peak with the discovery of the girl's unchastity. In a confused illogical way Dora linked the losing of her own virginity — however much it was not her fault — with Rose's shameless promiscuity. Both of them, as it were, had 'gone wrong' in her eyes. Now, nearing middle age, it had become more than she could bear.

Pauline, only vaguely aware of what ailed her mother, did her best. So did Ted who, knowing more, still had no knowledge about the letter his wife had seen, with all its salacious references to past intimacies and lewd suggestions about more to come. Dora had thrown it in the fire, had watched it brown, curl and finally crinkle into ashes, but the words seemed to have burnt into her brain so that most days she was unable to think of anything else.

Dr Evesham felt he had reached an impasse. He wanted Dora admitted to a wing of the local hospital which, although it took patients with mental troubles, had no connection with the asylum in which her mother had died. Nevertheless, Dora became more distressed. For the first time she showed a certain amount of spirit, saying nothing would persuade her to leave home. She then went on to make wild irrational assertions about people trying 'to put me away' and 'only over my dead body'.

Another Christmas passed, during which Rose had told her family, not quite truthfully, that she would be obliged to remain on duty throughout. It was this which caused Pauline, a little later in the New Year, to write to her elder sister. She said her mother's health had greatly deteriorated and she was scared. Her father was overworked and at the end of his tether. Dora was keeping him awake at night and he had had to relinquish all his duties as an air raid warden. Leslie had been called up and sometimes she wondered how long she herself could carry on. Might it not be possible for Rose to get a posting nearer home? She felt Dora was fretting at not seeing her.

Rose, having now acquired a second pip making her a full lieutenant, received the letter one morning when she was again going over to Hayling Island to take pay parade. She had been in a hurry and had left it unopened by her bed in the terraced house which had been commandeered by the ATS authorities. On her return that evening, she hastily changed into civilian clothes, as she was going off on a forty-eight hour pass with Commander Ross. As she left her room, she simply gathered up the letter and put it into a compartment of her handbag to read later.

It was not until after dinner at a hotel in the New Forest that she thought about it again. Even then, she did not open it. Matters more interesting were taking precedence. Phillip Ross, staring at her cleavage, suggested she might like to 'go on up' to the rooms he had booked for them both. It had been necessary to take a double and a single because identity cards and ration books made it difficult pretending to be man and wife.

Soon, Rose wearing a pre-war satin nightdress, which was hastily removed by her lover, was ensconced in a double bed in the larger room, ready to abandon herself to the pleasurable activity at which she excelled. Her sister's letter remained where it was, still unopened, until she returned to Portsmouth.

Back at Market Winton, Pauline had felt sure that Rose would have telephoned before the weekend. She had posted her letter on the Wednesday morning so that Rose would receive it at least by Friday. She went to bed that night puzzled and worn out by her mother's vagaries. On the Saturday Dora appeared more withdrawn than she had ever known her. Pauline longed for Rose to call because, much as she appreciated her father's support, she felt she needed to talk to someone of her own sex. Besides, he was working so hard and she knew that on Saturdays he was always late home, having been obliged to stay on to make up prescriptions after Dr Evesham's six p.m. surgery.

About two o'clock that afternoon Pauline, after settling Dora down for a rest and praying Rose would not telephone while she was out, took up the ration books and hurried to the shops. It was the only time of day she felt it was safe to leave her mother. Now, she almost ran to the butcher, hoping that the better cuts would not all have been snapped up earlier. It always intrigued her that although the Bassetts were treated ostensibly like everyone else according to the rationing regulations of the time, yet Mr Gurney invariably slipped a few extra bones into her parcel for Patch, their dog — or so he said. He was a kind man and she suspected that he knew she would boil them up to make some nourishing stock for her sick mother.

It did not occur to her to look in on Dora on her return. She had only been gone a few minutes and she hoped her mother might have been asleep. Quite often she did not appear downstairs again at all or, if she did, not until after Pauline had taken her up a cup of tea. When, as usual at half past four, she went upstairs with this, she found her parents' bed empty. Nor was Dora anywhere else in the house. Panic-stricken, she rang her father who shut up shop and came home at once. The police were called and all Pauline could now do was fix the blackout curtains and wait while they and her father went out searching for her mother.

The evening wore on. Patch, sensing her anxiety, came and sat beside her. Absentmindedly, she stroked the top of his head. A wind got up, whining round the house and rattling the windows as if it were angry with its occupants. All of a sudden, Patch threw back his head and let out a long high-pitched howl.

Pauline knew, then, that her mother would never come home. A hatred against Rose welled up inside her. If only she had telephoned, this might never have happened. *Why* had her half-sister ignored her letter?

Why indeed. At the very moment when Dora's body was recovered from the River Winn, at this time of the year in full flood, Rose was climaxing for the third time with Commander Phillip Ross.

Part Four

25

HER mother's suicide did something to Rose. That the other members of the family were deeply shocked and heartbroken, went without saying. But Dora's eldest daughter was, for the first time, acutely conscience-stricken. She had always known that she was the cause of her mother's illness, but she had never really allowed guilt to surface. Her character was such that she was able to keep her subconscious firmly under control. Even when the tragedy happened, she did not exactly allow the situation to overwhelm her, nor did it make her mend her ways with regard to the opposite sex. But it certainly started her thinking seriously again about something which had long been in the back of her mind: taking revenge on the family of her late father for the harm he had done to her mother. By doing that she felt she would somehow be exonerating her own responsibility for Dora's death. One day, she would track down his legitimate offspring, her unknown half-sister. Why should she sail through life probably spared any knowledge of her father's sin?

But with the war in its final years, Somerset House records still safely evacuated to Wales, her various postings to Halifax and Edinburgh — by which time she had been made a Junior Commander — and then to Germany after VE Day, Rose had little opportunity for pursuing her objective. Once again, it remained dormant, even though she was sure that, in the fullness of time, she would come face to face with the young woman who had been born and bred surrounded by all the advantages she herself had never known.

When Rose was finally demobbed in 1946, she returned to England, got herself a small flat with money she had accumulated — partly due to her own financial astuteness and partly due to various 'presents' over the years from countless admirers — and, thanks to her credentials and the personal recommendation of a Lieutenant General

239

for whom she had worked in Berlin, found herself a job in a publishing company in St James's.

Rose had never regarded herself as being particularly literary, but she knew she had a facility for fast reading, gathering relevant facts and typing them out in the form of a précis, which was more than helpful to anyone in whose service she was employed. She rarely now went back to Market Winton. With Dora's death, it seemed as if her position in the family was somehow nullified. Pauline was a fully-fledged hairdresser, Leslie was following in his father's footsteps and training to be a chemist. Ted, whenever she saw him, seemed increasingly grey and gaunt, a travesty of the man she remembered once having wondered what it would be like to sleep with. So far as she was concerned, she felt he had served his purpose — and then was conscience-stricken enough to feel mortified for the thought. That he and Dora were both better individuals than she could ever hope to be, she knew; but they were yesterday's people. They belonged to the past. She had no desire to emulate them. She was involved with a new way of life and, a little less urgently, with a certain person in particular whose path she was sure she would eventually cross.

In spite of the ravages which six years of war had inflicted on London, Rose found living there extremely stimulating and her job highly satisfying. Although her secretarial qualifications came in useful, she was by no means just a secretary but an assistant to one of the senior editors, an elderly man called Hugh Davenport. Most of the manuscripts submitted for publication were sent to outside readers, but he would sometimes give her one to read, especially fiction, for he recognised she seemed to have an unerring sense of what would appeal to women, especially those of her own generation. The heavier, more serious works did not interest her and, sensibly, Hugh never asked her to pass judgment on them.

One day, after she had been with the company a couple of years, he paused by her desk and said, "Rose, you were in the war. These poems have been sent to me by a Mrs Robson. I wonder if you'd take a look at them. They've been written by a young woman who evidently lost someone close to her, an air force pilot. They're very personal. Apparently the authoress does not wish to be named. I'd value your opinion, seeing that you're probably about the same age."

Poetry was not in Rose's line, but she was quite flattered to be asked to comment. She took the manuscript home with her and, it being one of the rare evenings when she happened not to be going out, read it straight through while eating her supper.

In spite of herself, Rose was moved. The poems had something, yet she was not quite sure what. But she could quite see why Hugh Davenport was interested in them. They would, of course, only make a slight volume, but that was all to the good, seeing how shortage of paper prevailed. Rose knew that the war, with all its privations and tragedies, was still very much in people's minds and she felt that anyone reading the poems could not fail to appreciate their sensitivity, sincerity and the sentiments behind them. Yet they were not sentimental. They reminded her of Alice Duer Miller's *White Cliffs*. She took them back to work with her next day and put them on Hugh's desk, with a concise report to that effect and was quite pleased when, sometime later, she heard that *Echoes* was to be published under the pseudonym *Andrea Viner*.

For such a slight publication by an unknown author it did quite well. There was a review in a national newspaper by an established poet, another in a Scottish periodical and, later on, a reprint of one of the poems in a monthly magazine. On the strength of this, Hugh Davenport was asked if Andrea Viner could be interviewed, but he was obliged to reply that it was not possible as the author disliked publicity. Scenting something of a mystery, the journalist persisted. Why were the poems published at all, he asked, if their author was so chary of revealing her identity? Hugh replied that this was a condition to which he had been forced to agree if the poems were to see the light of day.

Thereafter, interest in *Echoes* died down. Rose obtained a complimentary copy and put it in her bookcase along with several other books she had acquired. Her small home was beginning to mean more and more to her. When she felt she could afford it, she bought a picture or two. They were never very expensive, but she had become keen on enhancing her surroundings and establishing herself as a person who knew, or thought she knew, what was what. She had no wish to share this home of hers with any men, much as many a man seemed quite keen on sharing it with her. Often, she found herself explaining to some admirer that she had no interest in marriage or family life. If she happened to find an individual she fancied, then she would sleep with him; but her curiously detached, almost clinical, attitude to sex meant the relationship never went much further.

She had by now ascertained from Somerset House — re-established in London — a few more details about her father prior to the war. She knew he had married a woman called Elizabeth Forbes-Jamieson, the only daughter of Sir Charles and Lady Forbes-Jamieson of Meredith Place in Berkshire. The proximity of their home to her own had startled her and made her regret that she had not been more assiduous in her enquiries in the past. On receiving this new information she had made a special visit to Market Winton on the pretext of wanting to see how her stepfather and Pauline and Leslie were getting on. During the weekend, she had managed to ascertain that Lady Forbes-Jamieson and her husband had both died and that their daughter, who had been living in the district, had now remarried and moved away at the end of the war. Thereafter, the trail went dead.

By the time a second volume of verse by Andrea Viner arrived on Hugh Davenport's desk, Rose's determination to find her half-sister, had also somewhat evaporated owing to other more urgent considerations.

26

WHEN Elizabeth Kimberley married David Robson at the end of the war, she knew how much pleasure it would give her mother, then in failing health. She also knew that Gertrude, who was proposing to give up living in London, would accept the news fairly phlegmatically. But she was worried about telling her daughter. It was not that she thought Daphne would object in any way. It was just that Elizabeth was very conscious that while she herself had become the recipient of so much happiness, her daughter had missed out. She had lost the only young man with whom she had ever been in love.

Elizabeth had never been able to forget how she had failed Daphne by not being at home when the child had heard that Bill Ripley was missing, presumed dead. The fact that she herself had been off on an assignation with David somehow made it seem all so much worse. By the time she had returned to Alverton Lodge and the matron at the emergency hospital had been able to contact her, Daphne had spent thirty-six hours in a state of shock. Elizabeth had straightaway gone to collect her daughter and had brought her home, where she remained for several weeks. Their GP had managed to call as often as he could and arranged for some special visits from a colleague, rather more experienced with young patients who had suffered bereavement.

For there was no doubt that that was what Daphne was suffering from and Bill Ripley had meant a great deal more to her than Elizabeth had ever suspected. She found it heartbreaking when, one day, Daphne said, "I think I'd like to go up to Yorkshire and see Bill's parents. After all, they lost him, too." Yet another part of her mind knew that it was a good sign. It was the first positive move Daphne had made since the tragedy and, although Elizabeth worried about the girl taking the journey alone in her condition, she felt it was right and admired her daughter for her courage. When, a week later, Daphne returned and announced that she was ready to go back to the hospital, Elizabeth realised that, in her own quiet way, her daughter was somehow working out her own salvation.

But for the rest of the war there were no more young men for Daphne. She became an older version of her former self: shy and reserved, but with an added wisdom and maturity. Sensing that the girl wanted time alone, the matron arranged for her to be billeted on a retired chaplain and his wife, rather than sharing the crowded noisy nurses' quarters at the hospital and it was here, during whatever free time she had, that Daphne wrote the poems which eventually, thanks to her mother, found their way into print.

She had shown them to Elizabeth, diffidently, while spending a week's holiday with her and David who, since their marriage, had become market gardeners on a clifftop holding in Cornwall. Before Daphne had gone back to London, where she was now taking a full nurses' training at a teaching hospital, she had said to her mother, "I thought . . . you might like to read these. They're awfully personal. For your eyes alone. I wouldn't want anyone else to see them."

Elizabeth, touched and gratified, had taken them back to Penrock Farm after seeing Daphne off at Penzance station and read them straight through with the tears pouring down her face. Loyalty prevented her from showing them to her husband, much as she longed to do so. She had written to Daphne, saying that in her opinion the poems should not be kept in a drawer. She felt that they would help a great many people. Could she possibly give them to David to read and then, perhaps, set about getting them published.

At first, Daphne had been doubtful. But then she had telephoned to say, "I'm glad you liked them. I wouldn't mind your showing them to David. It would be wonderful if they were good enough to be printed. Then I'd be able to send a copy to Bill's parents. But I just don't want my name mentioned in any way."

It was David who hit on the idea of a pseudonym and Elizabeth had immediately gone to work. She felt as if, somehow, she was making a small atonement to this daughter of hers who had always meant so much to her.

After *Echoes* was published, Elizabeth hoped that Daphne might do more in the literary line, but it seemed as if her new — or, rather, her more exacting — work took up all her time and energy. Nevertheless, she was delighted when, a few years later, after Daphne had become a fully-fledged state-registered nurse, she discovered two things: one was that her daughter *had* actually written more verse but, even more exciting, another young man had come on the scene, a doctor called Nicholas Avery, a houseman in the hospital where Daphne worked.

The girl brought him down to Cornwall one weekend and, although younger than she was, he seemed all that Elizabeth and David could hope for in a possible future son-in-law: handsome, dedicated but with a lively wit, often teasing Daphne, though never unkindly, for her modesty and self-deprecation. "I tell her," he said to Elizabeth, "that she really must get rid of this anonymity complex," a sentiment with which, as her mother, she could only heartily agree. With difficulty, they persuaded Daphne that, even if she kept to the name of Andrea Viner, seeing that it seemed sensible after her small, even if only small, success, it would do no harm to reveal her true identity and become agreeable to a little more publicity.

Therefore, when Hugh Davenport received *Lifelines*, it was accompanied by a short explanatory letter, signed *Daphne Kimberley*, alias *Andrea Viner*. It was only by chance that the letter remained inside the manuscript when Hugh passed it over to Rose and, for at least two or three weeks she was too busy or, rather, too otherwise preoccupied, to take a look at it. A man had come into her life who, for the first time, made her think of matrimony.

Mark Wilson was fifty, rich, American and an art dealer. He was enough of a man of the world to see through all Rose's strategies in connection with the opposite sex straight away. She felt, in fact, that while fully appreciating her undoubted charms, he was silently laughing at her. She had never come across anyone quite like him and she was determined to make him fall for her. Much to her annoyance, Mark simply played her along.

When, eventually, she picked up *Lifelines* one evening when she had a feeling he was seeing some other woman, she was already in a bad mood before she retrieved the letter from the floor, where it had fallen on opening the manuscript. She was so preoccupied with what Mark could possibly be doing that, at first, she hardly noticed the double signature. When the name *Kimberley* suddenly registered, she sat there staring at it, a whole host of unrelated snippets of information which she had gathered from time to time now seeming to slot together in her mind like some jigsaw. *Kimberley*: her father's name. *Daphne*: a girl of roughly her own age. *Elizabeth*: the writer of the first letter, who could well have remarried a man called Robson. The poems themselves: one about a young child brought up by a widow, another about a deserted airfield, a third about a country house. It all added up. Here she was, sitting in judgment on the work of her half-sister. Feverishly, impatiently, Rose flipped through the contents of

Lifelines. Afterwards, she poured herself a drink, something which, of late, especially since the arrival of Mark Wilson, had become increasingly necessary to her.

Then she wrote her report: *These poems in no way come up to the standard of their predecessors. They are stereotype, cut-out cardboard efforts written with none of the freshness and appeal of* ECHOES. *I cannot recommend them as suitable for publication.*

All her pent-up frustration with Mark Wilson, her long-felt desire to hurt, humiliate and get even with her half-sister went into the penning of a few lines, which she attached to the manuscript and put on Hugh's desk the following morning.

On reading it, he was surprised and puzzled. It was strangely out of keeping with Rose's usual balanced well thought out criticisms. Studying the poems himself later that day he failed to understand why she should have condemned them so strongly, even vituperatively. It was almost as if she had some personal antipathy towards them. Before rejecting them out of hand, he asked another female colleague for a third opinion. The report came back that although *Lifelines* possibly did not have the immediacy of *Echoes*, the poems were more mature and showed remarkable depth of feeling. It could be that the earlier work had had a special saleability owing to the timing of its publication just after the war, but *Daphne Kimberley*, alias *Andrea Viner*, was certainly a young woman to watch.

Regretfully, Hugh Davenport decided to return *Lifelines* to its author. It was the mention of 'saleability' in the last report which tipped the scales. He was, after all, a publisher, not a philanthropist. He could not afford to take chances. He wrote what he hoped was a gentle let-down to an obviously extremely sensitive young woman, trusting that she would not take it too much to heart.

Although Daphne was, indeed, desperately disappointed, it was Nicholas Avery who was not only disappointed, but angry. Unbeknownst to Daphne, he made an appointment to see Hugh.

27

ON the day of Nicholas Avery's appointment with Hugh Davenport, which had been difficult enough to arrange owing to both men's commitments to their respective occupations, Hugh telephoned his secretary to say he was down with 'flu. Would she therefore cancel all his engagements. As the girl was unable to contact Dr Avery, who was already on duty, Rose was asked if she could help out.

Until then, she had been entirely unaware that the rejection of *Lifelines* had had any repercussions. When she heard that a Dr Avery had been coming to see her immediate boss about it, she was surprised and intrigued. Having rarely required the services of a doctor, they were, in Rose's mind, usually staid elderly individuals, such as Dr Evesham back at Market Winton. When this attractive young man appeared in her office later that day she was completely disarmed.

The previous evening Mark Wilson had stood her up, something which had never happened to her before. Nicholas Avery was like a lamb to the slaughter.

Inwardly still seething, she nevertheless gave him one of her most charming smiles, while noting three things: his incredible vitality, good looks and the probability that he was a virgin.

"You really wanted to see Mr Davenport, I understand," she began, once they were seated on either side of her desk. "I'm sorry he is unwell. I'm afraid you'll have to put up with me. What can I do for you?"

Nicholas Avery cleared his throat. He was caught off guard. Rather as Rose had imagined all doctors to be sober conservative individuals, so he had felt much the same about publishers. He found it difficult to believe that this devastatingly beautiful young woman had anything to do with what he thought of as a somewhat mundane trade. Rose, in her tight-fitting black polo-necked jumper, wearing a gold chain and long dangling earrings to match, seemed more like an actress which, had he then but known it, was another profession at which she might well have excelled. He liked the way her shining blonde hair was swept upwards on either side of a face in which two enormous blue eyes regarded him speculatively. It was the same kind of look which the nurses at the hospital had sometimes given him, but with Rose there was a hint of something different, a knowingness, as if she was well aware that she possessed hidden attributes which she might or might not, be prepared to offer. In spite of himself, Nicholas felt a surge of excitement.

However, keeping with an effort to the matter in hand, he replied, levelly, "I don't know if that would be possible. You see, I came to ask Mr Davenport why he rejected *Lifelines*. It seemed to me such an excellent follow-up to Miss Kimberley's first work."

To gain time, Rose lowered her eyelids and fiddled with a gold pencil on her desk. It was obvious that this was her half-sister's boyfriend. Since discovering Daphne's whereabouts and damning her latest effort, she had been biding her time. But now fate had certainly played into her hands. After a moment, she looked up again and said, "The decision as to whether or not to publish any book never rests with one person alone, Dr Avery. Sometimes we employ outside readers. Mr Davenport would have obtained opinions from several sources."

"Oh." Not knowing anything about the publishing world, Nicholas was slightly nonplussed, but he persisted. "Did *you* read *Lifelines*?" he asked.

"Yes, but I was not the only one, as I explained."

"But didn't you think it was good, as good or better than *Echoes*?"

Rose was equal to the question she had been expecting. "I think Miss Kimberley shows promise, Dr Avery, but poetry is extremely difficult to sell at the best of times."

She stared at him now and he felt there was something almost hypnotic in the way she was forcing him to stare back, as if she was throwing down some sort of challenge, even though he did not quite know what it was about. He had a sudden desire to make her less sure of herself, more vulnerable, to see her stripped of all her decorative fashionable accessories, naked perhaps.

Abruptly, he stood up. "Forgive me. I am wasting your time."

She rose also. "Not at all, Dr Avery. It's been a pleasure to meet you. I know that Mr Davenport . . . we . . . all think highly of Miss Kimberley's talent. I hope she will continue to write. Not just verse." She paused. "I'm wondering if perhaps you and she would care to call and see me one evening. At home. Off the record, so to speak."

Nicholas shook his head, annoyed to find he was embarrassed. "I'm afraid that wouldn't be possible. Miss Kimberley . . . Daphne . . . does not know that I have come here. She would be most upset if she did."

"I see." He turned towards the door, albeit slowly. She came round the desk. He had never seen such a perfect figure. Daphne's was good, but this woman's was superlative. "Then seeing that we are both so keen on promoting Miss Kimberley's work," she continued, "how would it be if you were to come alone? I could tell you what we feel the public is now after. Discuss the possibility of her changing course." She picked up a card. "Here is my address. You might care to think about it."

He went down the stairs, sweating. He was astute enough to be well aware that it was not Daphne's interests Miss Bassett was concerned about. He wished he had not interfered. It had been stupid of him, presumptuous. But he loved Daphne, or thought he did. He could not bear to see her hurt. He would try to make amends for such foolish behaviour. He would surprise her, take her out to dinner that evening. Then he suddenly remembered she was starting night duty. There would be no chance of that for a while, no chance at all. He felt confused and dispirited. In spite of working at the same hospital, it was odd how seldom they managed to meet.

Daphne was also feeling even more depressed that day. The rejection of *Lifelines* had been bad enough, but now the sudden call to go on nights was like an added setback. She knew, of course, that she would always have to do her share, but this time it had come round rather earlier than expected, due to so many nurses being off sick with influenza. At the best of times, Daphne had never taken kindly to working at night. She recalled her wartime duties at the emergency hospital and how she had always found it so difficult to sleep during the day. She was a little better at it now, but not much. The worst part was not being able to see Nicholas. It was maddening that their off duty times never seemed to coincide.

Down in Cornwall, Elizabeth also sensed the frustration in her daughter's last letter. She and David had been equally distressed on hearing that Daphne's second volume of verse had been rejected and they could only hope that the girl would find consolation in the support of Nicholas Avery, that nothing would go wrong this time with the loving relationship which they felt she so deserved.

But however much it might have been deserved and however much Nicholas Avery knew that Daphne deserved it, this was no defence against the forces of nature conspiring against them, the strongest forces in the world, which paid little attention to justice.

Nicholas had not been able to get Rose out of his mind. The card she had given him was like some kind of illegal passport to pleasure. A week later he telephoned her, as she had known he would. Nor did it take her long to seduce him, as she had also known would happen. But for Rose, while thoroughly enjoying the proceeding, there was an added frisson or, rather, two: she was redressing the situation vis-à-vis Mark Wilson, while ruining her half-sister's romance.

Her ability to do this appealed enormously to Rose's sense of power. The fact that Daphne, as yet, not only had no idea what was going on but, if and when she found out, might still not know the true identity of the woman who had stolen her boyfriend, made it all the more exciting. Stringing Nicholas Avery along, giving but sometimes withholding, sex was, to Rose, a splendid kind of sport, similar to that which anglers might enjoy when landing a large fish. True, Nicholas Avery was nowhere near as big a fish in the sense that Mark Wilson had been, but he was a quick learner and had soon known just how to please her.

For his part, Nicholas was entirely besotted. The times when Rose, for one reason or another, said she was unable to see him, made him consumed with jealousy. He imagined some other man feeling her move rhythmically beneath him as he brought her to orgasm, hearing her throaty whispers: "No ... wait ... yes ... *Now* ... " and then their entwined bodies reaching the final ecstasy. His rational mind knew that Rose was no good, that she wasn't fit to be in the same room as Daphne, but he was powerless to help himself. He lived for the days, but mostly nights, when he could get away from the hospital and climb the stairs to her flat, where she would open the door to him wearing, unless they were going out to dinner, something diaphanous, her long blonde hair, released from its daytime chignon, falling round her shoulders.

Sometimes afterwards, although he tried hard not to think about it because he felt guilty when making any comparisons between Rose and Daphne, he couldn't help wondering how he could possibly have become involved with two such dissimilar women. They were such poles apart. The only thing they had in common so far as he could see, was that they both had a mole — or beauty spot, as he believed they were called — in exactly the same place, high on the left cheekbone.

28

ELIZABETH had received several quite friendly letters from Gertrude since she had left London. It seemed as if she had become something of a rolling stone, trying out various locations in the British Isles before, as she put it rather dramatically, 'deciding where to end my days'. Meanwhile, she said she wanted to keep in touch with her 'nearest and dearest'.

The last phrase somewhat surprised Elizabeth. She had never connected Gertrude with having any nearest and dearest unless, of course, she counted Claud, when he was alive, on whom she realised her sister-in-law had doted. Could it be, Elizabeth wondered, that Gertrude was mellowing with age or simply very lonely. She must be well over sixty. It appeared that she particularly wanted to hear more about Daphne. Had she written any more verses? Gertrude often reiterated how much she had liked

Echoes, a copy of which her niece had been kind enough to send her.

Elizabeth had replied to Gertrude's latest letter saying that Daphne had, indeed, written a further volume but, sadly, it had been rejected for publication. She felt her daughter was, at present, rather depressed. Elizabeth wondered whether to tell Gertrude that Daphne had a new young man, but decided against it. The girl would not thank her for discussing her love life.

Gertrude had quickly replied, suggesting that if Daphne could get leave from the hospital might she care to accompany her on a trip to Scotland? It would do her good.

Daphne was apprehensive about the proposal, but at the same time eager for it to take place. It was therefore arranged that as soon as she came off night duty, when she would be due for ten days' holiday, she would join up with Gertrude on a sightseeing tour of Edinburgh followed by a trip to the Western Isles. Of late, Daphne had been unable to understand or find any reason for Nicholas's strange behaviour. She only knew that he simply seemed to be no longer in love with her. Having denied that he had found someone else and, because Daphne was a truthful person herself who never doubted any of her friends could possibly be otherwise, she found it all the more puzzling. The fact that Nicholas seemed positively keen on her going away when she had told him about it, was extremely galling.

"You seem glad to be getting rid of me," she said, one day when he had taken her out to lunch before she tried to get a few hours' sleep prior to going on night duty at eight p.m.

"Don't be silly, Daff." Her innocence, naïveté, irritated him. "I just hope you'll have a splendid time. You deserve it."

As soon as he had used the word 'deserve', he felt even more irritated, because it increased his own guilt. Daphne was *so* deserving and he simply wasn't. He wished he hadn't lied about there not being anyone else. It would make it all the more difficult when he was obliged to tell her. With all his heart he wanted Daphne to be happy, as long as she was happy with some other man. The

267

trouble was she was so single-minded. He had initially been attracted by that: her dedication to the job in hand which made her such a good nurse, her compassion, her sweetness, her obvious adoration of him which had boosted his ego. But now he found it cloying. Daphne just wasn't sexy. After Rose, who had made a man of him, there was simply no question of going on with Daphne. If only some other chap would come along. Sadly, he doubted it. She was a one-man girl all right. That was why she had taken so long to get over her previous and, apparently, only love affair. Once she had fallen in love she had no eyes for anyone else.

Unlike Rose. Even now, this minute, while he was doing his best to jolly Daphne along, part of Nicholas's mind was wondering whether Rose was distributing her favours elsewhere. The thought was unbearable. After he had dropped Daphne off at the nurses' home, he determined he would try to see Rose that evening even though she had said she wasn't feeling too well. He had imagined this was simply an excuse. At

11 p.m., when he came off duty, he went round to the apartment block where she lived and rang the bell of her flat. For a while there was no reply. Stepping back, he looked up and realised that there was no light in her bedroom window. Then, suddenly, it lit up and a woman's voice on the intercom, sounding unlike Rose's, whispered hoarsely, "Yes? Who is it?"

"It's me, Nick," he replied and, to his surprise, was rewarded by the sound of the buzzer being pressed which automatically let him in. For once, he thought, as he climbed the stairs, Rose had not been lying.

"I've got 'flu," she said, abruptly, as soon as he entered her front door. "Better not to come too close."

"I'm terribly sorry."

"Don't be. I have a tough constitution. It won't last long. I'll be quite all right in a day or two."

"But why . . . didn't you let me know?"

"Have you forgotten? I did. I told you I wasn't feeling too good. Now just you leave me alone."

But he followed her into the bedroom,

where she got back into bed, pulled the eiderdown up around her and closed her eyes. Even in illness, Rose managed to look tantalisingly seductive. When he made no move to go, she opened her eyes and said, "Run along, Nick. Give my half-sister a break."

He stared at her, frowning. Half-sister? Who on earth was she referring to? She must be delirious, worse than he thought. She hadn't known what she was talking about.

"Look. I'm going out to an all night chemist. You need medicine."

"If you come back, I shan't answer the bell." He bent to kiss her, but she waved him away. "Just *go*, Nick. There's a good boy."

On his way down the stairs, the phrasing of her dismissal rankled. Was that all she thought of him? Admittedly, she was five years older than he was, but it hadn't seemed to matter. In fact, he had felt that it had been the other way round. Or was it Rose who had been clever enough to make him feel that? He became frantic with worry about their relationship. It had seemed so perfect, but tonight she had treated him as if he were a spoilt child. Of course, she wasn't well. Not herself. He must make allowances. That reference to her half-sister was most peculiar.

Once back in his rooms he went to bed but he was quite unable to sleep. Then, suddenly, at two a.m., he sat up. Already overwrought, he felt as if his mind was going into overdrive. Although in character no two women could have been less alike, yet physically perhaps there *was* a similarity between them. Both were tall. Both had good figures, Rose the more voluptuous. Daphne's would be better if she could put on weight, but she had told him that she had never been able to do that when she had lost so much after her pilot officer had been killed. Rose was the fairer of the two, but it suddenly came to him that the blondeness might have come out of a bottle or, at least, been assisted by it. But there was no doubt that they shared one unmistakable feature: that mole on both their left cheeks. As soon as Rose was better, he thought he might talk to her about it.

He did not, in fact, bring up the subject until some time later, when Daphne was away with Gertrude. Even then, he did not quite know how to go about it. In the end, it was Rose who actually gave him a lead.

"Have you heard from Daphne?" she asked, one evening when he had called for her at work on one of the rare occasions he had been able to leave the hospital earlier than usual. They were walking through St James's Park. The warmer weather had come, the daffodils were out and the influenza epidemic which had laid so many people low, including Rose, was over.

"No," he replied. He was both pleased and sorry, pleased that he would not be obliged to reply, sorry that it was obvious Daphne had been hurt.

They stood for a moment watching two ducks mating. It made him feel randy. "Let's get on," he said. They were on their way back to her flat. But Rose appeared to be in no hurry. "Why don't we sit down on that seat over there," she suggested. "I've got something to tell you." As she led the way, he followed, annoyed with her, annoyed with himself for always seeming to accede to her wishes.

"I'm leaving for Australia next week," she began, as soon as they were seated. "I'm going to work in Sydney in one of our branches out there."

He stared at her. "But you *can't*."

"Of course I can. It'll be good experience. It's settled. Hugh Davenport has made all the arrangements."

He took hold of both her arms, forcing her to look at him. "How long do you intend to be gone?"

She shrugged. "I don't know. Depends if I like it down under. I might decide to stay permanently."

He tightened his grip so that she winced slightly. "But why?" he almost shouted. "For God's sake, *why*?"

She told him then, everything. The park became deserted. "I'm a bastard," she said, "in more ways than one. I imagine I was probably conceived not less than half a mile from here. My mother never would tell me much. But, gradually, I got hold of the story. I put two and two together. I always vowed that one day I'd make my half-sister suffer, just as my mother must have suffered. Well, I've done it, haven't I? It was I, more than anyone else, who was responsible for *Lifelines* being rejected. Then I soon saw I was in a position to deal Daphne another blow. I'm a bitch. I put paid to her romance with you. I'm no good, Nicholas Avery. No bloody good at all. My only hope is to make a fresh start. The other side of the world. I always thought I'd confront Daphne one day. Watch her face as I told her she was my half-sister. But that's not important any more. You see, I've realised she must be a very nice person, who knows nothing about me. All these years I've thought of her as having everything. Everything I didn't. I wanted to take that away from her. I don't want to any more. I don't even want to meet her. I've done her enough harm. But I suppose . . . for you and her . . . it's too late."

"Yes," he replied, slowly. "I'm afraid it's too late." Then he got up and walked away.

Epilogue

DURING the summer of 1993, two elderly grey-haired ladies were at the same literary luncheon in the West End of London. One was a celebrated authoress, the other a visitor from New South Wales, accompanied by a rugged-looking escort. The women were not seated anywhere near each other. The authoress, in whose honour the luncheon was being given, was at the long top table from where, later on, she would be speaking about her autobiography which had just been published. The other woman was sitting at a small table at the back of the room, aware that her companion was not enjoying the proceedings, for which she had gone to enormous trouble to obtain tickets.

After coffee had been served, the loyal toast drunk and the authoress introduced to the assembly by another well-known writer, Andrea Viner stood up — with difficulty because she was severely crippled by arthritis — and began her address. Her voice, though soft and controlled, carried astonishingly well and the sheep farmer, accompanying the woman at the back, stopped being bored and began to listen.

The authoress began, somewhat surprisingly, by bringing up the subject of Rejection. She said that she did not think it was necessarily all that bad a thing. She described how, in her youth, she had been an aspiring poetess, but her second volume of verse had been rejected by her publishers, at the same time as she had suffered another rejection through an unhappy love affair. This double blow had made her lose all confidence in her writing and herself. She had never sent the verses elsewhere but had hidden them in the back of a drawer, rather as she had hidden herself from life. Some years later she had come across the verses again and the title poem had given her the idea for a novel. When this, much to her amazement, had been accepted for publication and turned out to be a success, she felt that perhaps the rejection of her second volume of verse had been a blessing in disguise, in much the same way as the more personal rejection. "I doubt I would ever have made a good wife or a good poet," she said.

"I am a great believer in fate," Andrea Viner went on. "I was very grateful to find, in middle age, the vocation I believe I subconsciously always wanted. I turned to the verses again for an idea for my second novel, and yet again for my third. I came to the conclusion that, like seeds in the ground, they had all along merely been waiting for the opportunity to grow into something bigger and, I hope, better. That was why I called my autobiography *Keeping It Dark*.

Andrea Viner did not talk for long, but it was a gentle, unusual and rather disarming little speech. She was duly thanked by the chairman and then an official announced that copies of *Keeping It Dark* were available for purchase on the top table, where Miss Viner would be happy to sign them.

Rose immediately jumped up and went to buy one, much to the sheep farmer's surprise. He knew that she had worked in a publisher's office before she had come to live with him, and that she always looked forward to the day when the mobile library came round and she could change her books. He was not much of a reader himself but, if it kept her happy, then so much the better. He realised that she missed the life in Sydney and had possibly regretted shacking up with him. That was why he had suggested that they should take a trip to England. He was frightened of losing her. He couldn't live without a woman and, after his wife had died, he had visited Sydney for the express purpose of finding another one.

That had been ten years ago. He had picked Rose up in a hotel. She had still been good-looking, albeit rather on the heavy side, but he had always liked a woman with a bit of flesh on her. Not being experienced in the ways of the opposite sex, he had imagined her blonde hair was natural. He had admired her exuberance. He felt that she looked healthy, as if she was capable of plenty of hard work. She was certainly more than a match for him in bed.

Rose, at that time, was actually at a crossroads. She had been obliged to retire from her job to make way, as they said, for younger staff. Although she still had men friends, she realised that her 'pulling power', as she thought of it, was by no means as great as it once had been. Charlie Morgan seemed to be the answer to the situation. She felt he was basically a sound man who would take care of her. But she stuck to her lifelong decision never to marry. There was no knowing that someone else might come along, nor that she might find a sheep station in the outback too lonely.

She had therefore agreed to live with Charlie and, up to a point, had kept her side of the bargain. She cooked and cleaned, after a fashion, and accommodated him in bed whenever he so desired and even, at other times, made him accommodate her. But being miles from the nearest hairdresser, her hitherto blonde hair soon turned grey while, possibly due to boredom, she ate — and drank — rather more than she should, so that her well-preserved figure ballooned.

Now, as Charlie watched her waddle towards the top table, he wondered, not for the first time, what she was up to. He had never understood her. She had always refused to talk about her past. Sometimes, fancifully, he even wondered whether she had some criminal record which had made her emigrate to Australia back in the 1950s. The fact that she had been so keen to come to this particular luncheon must surely have meant that this Andrea Viner woman, whoever she was, had figured in Rose's life at some period.

He watched her queuing up now at the top table, getting out her notecase to pay for the book which evidently meant something to her. When, eventually, Rose stood in front of Andrea, he would have been even more curious had he been able to hear their conversation.

"I should be grateful," Rose said, passing the authoress her book, opened at the title page, "if you would sign . . . well, *inscribe* this for me."

"But, of course." Daphne Kimberley, *alias* Andrea Viner, looked up and smiled. She was quite used to such requests from perfect strangers. "Please tell me your name and if there is anything special you would like me to write?"

There was a momentary, but only momentary, hesitation. Then the authoress's half-sister replied, "Perhaps you would kindly just put 'To Rose'." She felt almost like asking her to add, 'For keeping it dark', but quickly thought better of it.